The Quarter Horse

The Horse
Rescuers Series
Book 4

Patricia Gilkerson

Published by
Fire and Ice
A Young Adult Imprint of Melange Books, LLC
White Bear Lake, MN 55110
www.fireandiceya.com

Cover Art by Stephanie Flint

The Quarter Horse is dedicated to my husband Jim, who admires and respects the breed, and who explained the difficulties of treating a colicky horse. I would also like to dedicate this to Ivy, the newest of my grandchildren, who won't be able to help loving horses.

Chapter One

~ Breakout ~

Loud hoof beats in the yard. I put down my lemonade and ran to the window. Three adult horses and a colt milled around in Miss Julie Applegate's backyard. The six-foot wide aluminum gate hung open.

"Oh, no! Jeff, didn't you close the gate?"

"I thought I did," he said, setting down his physics book and standing up.

My mouth went dry. There is nothing scarier to a horse owner than the sound of hoof beats where there aren't supposed to be any. It means horses are loose and loose horses like to run. And run. A potential disaster if they ran down the long driveway and got onto the highway to town. Disasters like that might show up on the evening news, complete with images of ambulances, cops, and dead horses. If we could just ease them back into their paddock, maybe they wouldn't start running.

"Hurry! We have to get them back in. You walk toward them by the barn while I go around the other side of the yard. Maybe they'll head back into the paddock. Just don't spook them so they start running!"

Hoping beyond hope that the horses would stay calm, I walked past them in the yard of the old white house, trying to head them away from the driveway and back into their pasture. The horses tossed their heads and started trotting around, just now realizing they were free. Jeff waved his arms, but that made them wilder.

"No! Don't scare them!" I yelled at Jeff as, nostrils wide, the horses began to gallop. Dotty, the smallest and bossiest of the three adult horses, ran right past me up the half-mile dirt driveway toward the main highway. The others followed, gaining speed.

Clattering on the gravel drive, the horses and colt disappeared over the hill, neighing to each other. They sounded like they were having a party, but I had chills, thinking of them running down the busy highway toward Serendipity Springs, the nearest town. My horses might easily be galloping to their death. Could we catch them? We had a chance if they would slow down and graze. I ran into the barn and grabbed three halters. There was one for each adult horse. The colt would follow his mother, if we could only catch her.

Who was around to help us? I ran through the list in my head as I hurried to Jeff. My best friend Addie was out of town. My dad was at work and it would take him too long to get here. Miss Julie was too old to chase horses and she was gone on an errand anyway. It was up to me and Jeff. I handed him a halter and lead, and we ran up the drive after the horses.

"Piper, should I go back and shut the gate or get the truck?" Jeff panted as he ran. He's thin and tall, but not very athletic.

"No and no," I said, "We would just have to leave the truck and we'll need the gate open for when we bring them home. We might need the truck later to find them." I prayed that wouldn't happen.

We ran together down the lane that was the long driveway to Miss Julie's farm. Addie and I kept our horses there and we liked to visit with Miss Julie in her big white farmhouse. Jeff lived there with Miss Julie until his graduation from high school in the spring. The mare and foal belonged to him, but he wasn't into horses and never really paid enough attention to closing gates and such. It drove me crazy, since I was the one who ended up taking care of them. That's what happened when I depended on him to do things.

As we ran, Jeff muttered things like, "Can't believe I did that," and "So stupid," really beating himself up.

"Jeff! It's done!" I said. "Let's just catch them and you can call yourself names later!"

He sighed and we ran on. As we came over the crest of a small hill, we were met by the four horses trotting back toward us. One POA— Pony of the Americas—that was spotted all over, one gray half-Arabian gelding, and one bay Quarter horse mare with her look-alike colt; all accounted for. This was encouraging. Maybe I could catch them.

"Here honey, here sugar," I called to the pony in a soft voice, and held my hand out, trying to slow Dotty down and maybe get a halter on her. Their taste of freedom made them goofy and they acted like naughty children. Heads high, tails in the air, they snorted and pranced past us as if they were kids running away from school. I imagined them saying "Haha! Can't catch me!" Way down where the driveway meets the road, Miss Julie had seen that the horses were loose, and blocked their escape by turning her car sideways. They had turned and trotted back the way they came. What an awesomely smart old lady! Now the horses were still loose, but at least they'd be contained in the fenced yard and couldn't get out on the main road.

"Oh, boy! Thanks, Miss J!" Jeff called to her as we turned and trudged back to the house, breathing heavily. Miss Julie waved back at him, got in her car, and drove slowly behind us to the yard. Reaching it, she parked sideways again, blocking the drive so they couldn't escape.

My sense of panic was over, but we still needed to get them back in the fenced paddock by the barn. They trotted, snorting, around the yard.

"I'll take Nickel," I said, referring to the tall grey Arabian. "He'll be the easiest to catch. You see if you can get Daisy. The colt will follow her." I dropped one of my two halters on the ground and walked slowly toward Nickel with the other halter hidden behind my back.

"Hey, Nick. Hey, son." I sounded like my dad, who called all girl horses Sis and all boy horses Son. Most people I knew who worked with horses did that.

"Come on, it's okay." I held my hand out as if I had a carrot in it. I didn't have a treat this time, but much as I love them, horses really aren't

3

very smart. You can fake them out easily.

Nickel settled down and nibbled grass with his good eye on me. He was blind in one eye, but was just the sweetest horse ever. His head came up as I approached and his nose lifted to sniff at my hand.

"Good boy!" I whispered, easing the lead rope over his neck and collecting the end. He was now as good as caught, with his head in a loop of rope. That done, it was a simple thing to draw the halter over his nose, up around his ears and buckle it. I rubbed Nickel's neck for allowing me to catch him. As I held the lead rope, he snorted at me and rubbed his nose on my shoulder. I sighed and looked around to see what Jeff was doing. He walked toward Daisy, halter at his side. Every time he got close, she moved away, staying about two arms' lengths away from him, her shiny red coat gleaming in the sun. The six-month old colt, Dancer, followed his mom as she led Jeff around the yard. Dotty the pony was sniffing Miss Julie's petunias by her porch, eyeing us without much interest. Miss Julie had taken up a post by her car, in case any of the horses tried to sneak past it.

"Aargh!" said Jeff, who had more patience with his guitar than his horses.

"See if they'll follow us," I called. I turned and led Nickel through the big gate into the small paddock between the barn and house. I walked him all the way in, toward the big oak tree that grew in the center of the field. Slowly, like a parade, my wayward horses followed, the grey gelding with me, with the spotted pony, the bay mare and the colt bringing up the rear. I was thankful that horses were herd animals and wanted to stay together.

Relieved to have everyone where they belonged, I called, "Close the gate, Jeff. And this time, latch it!" It came out a little sharper than I meant.

He pulled the gate shut hard and stalked up to the house. I took off Nickel's halter and hugged his neck. I walked over to Dotty, the innocent-looking pony, and patted her on her spotted neck. Daisy walked over to us, sniffing for treats, so I rubbed her forehead and kissed her, gazing into her huge brown eyes. None of them looked a bit sorry for their adventure. I smiled and left the runaways happily nibbling clover. The disaster was over—no harm done. I took a huge deep breath in relief and walked out the gate and up to Miss Julie's house.

Jeff and I flung ourselves into our usual places in Miss Julie's rocking chairs on the wide front porch. I had the half-grown cat, Willie Nelson, on my lap. Miss Julie was inside making some celebration lemonade. Jeff rocked quickly, as if something bothered him. I wondered what he was antsy about. Easter was coming in a few days and we were on our spring break. The excitement was over so why didn't he relax now? I slumped in my chair, exhausted.

"So Piper…"

"Mmm Hmmm?" My eyes were closed in relief from having stopped a disaster.

"You didn't have to snap at me."

"When?" I sat up and stared.

"When you told me to shut the gate. I mean, I know I was an idiot to leave it open, and I feel terrible about it, but I didn't do it on purpose."

"I didn't snap at you!"

"Well, yes, you did. And you didn't have to."

"I did not snap at you. I only told you to shut the gate and latch it."

"It was the way you said it." Why was he being so sensitive? Jeff was a senior, while I was only a sophomore. We went out together sometimes. Well, we had twice. Okay, he was my first real date. The Homecoming Dance was fun and we had a good time. We were friends, but it felt like he was always telling me how to say things. Since the dance, we had gone to one movie and that was it. I wasn't sure how he felt about me…or how I felt about him. Didn't he want to go out with me anymore? I definitely wanted to go out with him again, but always got cold feet when I thought about doing the asking myself. "Hey, I'm sorry if I said it wrong. I just don't want the horses to get out. What if they ran out onto the highway and got hit by a car? Or lost? Or stolen? Not good, Jeff, not good. You know if you don't want Daisy you should sell her."

"Yeah, well, I am going to sell her."

"What?"

"I need the money for college."

"Why didn't you tell me?"

"Look, I know you love those horses, all of them. Even mine. But I'm going to need some money and the horses are all I have to sell. I didn't tell you sooner because I knew you'd be upset."

"Both of them? Seriously? Even if you get a scholarship?"

"Even if. There are all kinds of expenses that a scholarship won't cover. I can't sell the truck—I'll need it for getting around. And I have to buy insurance for it and a bunch of other expenses. So I have to sell the horses."

That was bad news, having to sell that beautiful mare and her colt, but maybe they were worth a lot of money.

"Here we go! Nice cold lemonade for the Horse Rescuers. You just rescued them all over again." Miss Julie was probably the most cheerful woman I'd ever known. She was the one who helped Addie and me rescue our two horses, and let us keep them in her barn. Holding three large glasses, she came out of the kitchen trailed by Honey, her sheltie.

"Miss Julie," I said, "you were the one who rescued them when you pulled your car into the driveway so they couldn't run down the highway. Jeff and I just caught them and got them in the paddock. You're a Horse Rescuer, too."

We dropped the subject of selling the horses. Jeff didn't seem like he wanted to talk about paying for college in front of Miss Julie. I still wanted to make sure he wasn't so careless anymore, but decided to let it go for now. We both took a tall glass of lemonade and drank.

"Piper," said Miss Julie, sitting down on her porch swing. "What do you hear from Addie?"

"She's having a fun time in Wisconsin. Her dad took her to visit some of his friends and she met a cute guy that she's drooling over. She'll be home Sunday, late."

"Drooling?" asked Jeff, with his eyebrows raised.

"Well, every other text is about Joe. Joe, Joe, Joe."

"I heard your dad is hiring another veterinarian to work in his clinic," said Miss Julie.

My jaw dropped and the lemonade glass nearly did.

"Where did you hear that?" Nothing, I mean *nothing* happens with my dad's vet clinic without me knowing about it. He tells me everything and even asks my opinion sometimes. I used to go on farm calls with him. I don't go so much anymore since I have school and the horses and all, but I still help him order medicine, and magazines for the waiting room. When I was little, I liked to take old copies of *Horse and Rider* and cut out pictures of the horses I liked best.

Miss Julie looked innocent. "I overheard it at the clinic this morning when I took Honey in for her rabies shot. But maybe it was just gossip."

Hmmm. I needed to talk to Dad and find out what was going on. Dad was too busy and actually did need to hire another vet to take some hours. I just wanted to be sure it was someone we all liked and got along with. Serendipity Springs, Kentucky is a small town.

"Well, gotta bounce," I said, standing and stretching. I had my bike with me, so it wouldn't take long to get to Dad's clinic.

"Let us know what you find out," said Jeff with a grin. He knows me—I couldn't pass up a chance to find out more. He smiled, so maybe he wasn't still mad at me. I patted Honey and Willie Nelson, waved goodbye and left.

Chapter Two

~ Getting the Facts ~

It was a short ride to my dad's office, the Serendipity Springs Veterinary Clinic. I propped my bike in the back against the building next to Dad's green pickup and Sue's tan minivan. Sue, Dad's receptionist and assistant, was my babysitter when I was little and when I was old enough, I babysat her two-year old boy when she needed me. If Dad was busy, Sue would tell me what was going on.

I walked in through the lab in back, past microscopes and bottles of pills, and was immediately hit by a wave of noise from the front room. Dogs barked, people yelled, and kids cried. Looking over the reception desk to the waiting room, I saw two large dogs, a German shepherd and a pit bull type barking at each other. The man and woman holding their leashes didn't seem to know what to do, so they just yelled at the dogs. A little girl, obviously scared of the barking and yelling, cried in a corner next to the magazine table.

Sue poked her head out of an exam room. "Piper! I'm *so* glad you're here. Will you take whoever's next into the other exam room ASAP? I can't leave this cat and your dad is in surgery." She closed the door again and was gone.

"So, who was here first?" I asked the two people with the dogs.

"I was," snarled the large man with the pit bull, checking his watch. His sleeveless shirt hung open in front and a wave of body odor washed over me.

"Want to bring your dog into this room?"

"About time, but you don't look like no vet," he said.

"I'm not the vet," I said, trying for patience with his rudeness and bad grammar. "Why don't you come in here? I'm sure my father will see you as soon as possible."

The man pulled his grumbling dog into Exam Room 2. I closed the door behind him and checked the other room to see how Sue was doing. She had finished with the kitty and was putting it into a cage in the cat kennel area.

"Whew, what a crazy morning! Thanks, Piper. How are you, honey?" she asked. I liked Sue—she was real and since I've started babysitting for her, she has never treated me like a kid, even though at thirty, she is twice my age.

"I'm pretty good," I said. "Miss Julie said Dad hired a new vet. Is that right?"

"Yes, thank God! It's just been nuts around here and getting worse every week."

"Who did he hire?"

"Some guy who can start next week. Can't be too soon!" Sue washed her hands and turned to me, grinning. "I didn't meet him, but I saw him leaving. He's real tall and redheaded." She wiggled her eyebrows and I had to smile. Sue is a single mom and looking for love.

"Why didn't Dad tell me?"

"Oh, honey, it all happened so fast! Your dad got a phone call, the guy drove out here to talk to him, and he was hired. I guess he was working in Louisville when he got laid off, and heard Dan was looking to hire someone."

"Will Dad be in surgery long?" I knew not to poke my head in and bother him there.

"I'll check, but he's got those two dogs to see when he comes out."

"Well, I'm going over there for dinner. I'll just talk to him tonight." I stayed at my dad's a couple of nights a week, but I mostly lived at Mom's house, especially on school nights. They've been divorced a few years now, but got along when they had to, like when I got in trouble. That happened more often than any of us liked.

"By the way, Piper, how is Jean doing? Does she still like working at the law office?"

"She does. She even sings on her way to work sometimes."

I had to smile, thinking about Mom and her job working for Miss Julie's son, Sam. They were dating and I wasn't sure whether it was the job or Sam that was making Mom so happy. I didn't really care which; it was just nice to have her feeling so good again.

As I said goodbye to Sue, I saw that the bulletin board in the waiting room was filled with index cards. It was covered with homemade ads for dogs, horses, free kittens, and little knitted doggie sweaters. Thinking that someone should weed them out, but not me, I slipped out the door. I got on my bike and headed home. On the short trip from the clinic, my phone doodled with a text from Addie, so I had to stop so I could read it.

JOE HATES ME!!!!

WHY?

THINKS I'M A DORK!

WHAT HAPPENED?

I BUMPED INTO HIM--MADE HIM SPILL HIS COKE ALL OVER HIS NEW GUITAR! HE WAS SO MAD!!

GUITAR?

YES! HE'S SO COOL AND IN A BAND.

HOW OLD?

20

DUDE, TOO OLD! WHAT DOES YR DAD SAY?

HE DOESN'T KNOW N U CAN'T TELL MY MOM!!!!
!?!?!?!?!

I KNOW BUT AFTER THIS WEEK I'LL NEVER SEE HIM AGAIN ANYWAY.):-(GOTTA GO-SEE YA

This was Thursday, and I would see Addie in three more days, four at the most. She was usually pretty common-sense about things, but she got kinda goofy about boys. Face it, she will flirt with anything in pants, but she's my only real friend and I needed her to come home.

Okay, Jeff was a friend, too, but that was different. He was the one I needed to talk to Addie about. I didn't know where things stood with us. I knew I was hung up on him, but he didn't always think about what he was doing and that made me crazy. His mind was always in his books, or his latest music. Sometimes he could be an idiot. Probably the best thing *was* for him to sell his horses. Addie might have been goofy about boys, but she was very sharp about other people's relationships.

Wondering what to do about Jeff, I walked into the house.

"Anybody home?" No answer. Mom was still at work with Sam. The law office was really busy that spring and Mom was working more hours than ever.

I grabbed a soda, flopped on the couch and turned on the TV. Middle of the day, nothing to watch. I clicked it back off, just as Mom came in.

"Piper! You're back!"

"Yeah, I didn't have anything to do."

"What about Jeff and the horses?"

I filled her in on the runaway fiasco we had earlier. I tried to explain it, but she's not a horse person, so she can't appreciate how close we all came to total disaster. "Mom, did you know your hair is messed up and your lipstick is smudgy?"

"Oh, geez," she said, running to a mirror. She ducked into the bathroom off the family room. When she came out a few minutes later, she was all tucked in and neat.

"I don't know how I got so messy!"

I decided not to say anything. It was her business, what she and Sam did at work. It was kinda funny that she thought I wouldn't know they were all huggy and kissy. I'd seen them together when they thought I wasn't around. After all, they'd been dating now for nearly a year.

"Did you know Dad hired a new vet?"

"I did. He called, looking for you, and told me. I guess your phone was off."

"No, sometimes it still doesn't work out at the farm. At least he tried to call me. It seems like everyone knows but me."

"I'm sure he'll call later. He's just so busy. Remember, that's why he hired someone new. That's why we couldn't.... oh, never mind."

"Why you couldn't what, Mom?" Even though I was cool with the divorce, I still needed answers, even after two years.

"Oh, Piper, we just couldn't get time for ourselves. We never had an evening together, never could concentrate on talking things out when we had disagreements. That's part of what went wrong." Mom was pacing now.

"Oh." I found myself in a rare place. Nothing to say. But I wondered to myself if Mom and Sam planned to get married.

"But it's better this way. We both have interesting jobs. We have a social life—well at least I do. And we both have you whenever we need you, or you need us." Mom smiled a big fake smile.

"Are you and Sam okay? Still together?" I couldn't believe I asked this, but I did.

Mom sat down and sighed. "Yes, we are. Sam is lovely—smart, funny, and thoughtful," she said and gave me a real smile.

"And he's totally cute," I added.

My mother laughed. "And he's totally cute," she agreed. "I just don't know where it is going."

As I thought of Jeff, that made two of us.

Chapter Three

~ Redheaded Stranger ~

I spent the early afternoon reading in my room, but after several hours, got tired of it. Mom was on an organizational tear, meaning she pulled things out of cupboards, tossed some of them and replaced what was left more neatly. I wanted nothing to do with that activity. Looking at my old collection of Breyer horses from when I was a kid reminded me of my own small herd of living, breathing, flesh-and-blood horses. I grabbed my phone and headed out the door. May as well go to the barn and see what the naughty nags were up to.

"Piper! Where are you going?" Mom can usually hear me going out, even from the back bedroom.

"To the farm. I'm eating at Dad's tonight, so I'll see you tomorrow."

"Okay, 'bye!"

I walked this time. It was still a beautiful spring day and I liked to think while I walked or rode. I thought mostly about the horses. Dotty and Nickel were mine and Addie's, but I considered Jeff's two horses part of my herd, too. They were always together and I took care of them.

As soon as I got there, I walked into the paddock to see my charges. Nickel came right over to me, blowing through his nose and looking for treats. He turned his head so his good eye could see me. I gave him a carrot, which he munched, then drooled orangey slobber on my hand. Wiping it on his back, I looked around for Dotty. That pony was cute as a bug, but kinda ornery. She bucked a little at first when you rode her, which scared Addie. We had rescued Dotty together, but then we had to find Addie a horse, too, so we could ride together. That was when we rescued Nickel.

Dancer, the six month-old colt, came trotting over to sniff me, but Daisy kept her distance. I wished that Jeff would put in some time petting her and handling her so she was used to people. Her previous owner, Jeff's stepmother, was a flake that knew and cared nothing about horses. She had won the mare in a poker game was how I heard it.

Looking around, I saw Jeff sitting on the front porch of the big old house, reading. Giving Nickel one last pat, I went through the fence and up to the house.

"Hey," I said. Was he still mad? Still upset with me?

"Hey, yourself."

Jeff put down his book, *The Martian Chronicles*, by his favorite author, Ray Bradbury. He really was cute, with his dark hair that needed trimming and his hazel eyes. He had somehow gotten better looking in the last six months since I met him. I had noticed girls at school watching him.

"Reading for school?"

"Yeah, I have a book report due. I'm just snowed under with work. No break for me, whine, whine." Jeff smiled—he had a nice way of never feeling sorry for himself. Especially since he had gotten a pretty raw deal out of life. And he did have a really great smile.

"So, are you still mad at me?" I asked, wanting things out in the open.

"I just don't know why you had to snap at me. I don't like it."

"Well, I didn't mean to! It just came out that way. I was freaked out about the horses getting loose, and besides, I said I was sorry."

"Well, maybe you should think before you say things." He wasn't going to let this go. "You know, you do it to Addie, too."

"So how about those Cardinals?" I tried to change the subject. "Hey, Jeff... about selling Daisy and Dancer...how long have you been thinking about it?"

"Are you kidding?" he said. "Only ten times a day for weeks. I can't afford to pay for their food and board, and I can't keep sponging off Miss Julie. I just don't have time to do anything about it. I have to get A's so I can get a scholarship to a good school and every minute I'm not studying I work for Mr. Simpson at school or do chores for Miss Julie."

"Jeez, Jeff, I didn't realize you were so busy."

"Have you seen me sitting around strumming the guitar lately? Or reading for fun?"

"Well, no... I guess I've been goofing off while you've been working."

"Miss Julie's been so great, letting me live here and all, I need to prove to her that I'm serious about school. I need to get my degree and pay her back somehow, but right now I've got to stop taking advantage of her. Those are purebred horses and your dad tells me they could be worth a lot."

"How much?"

"Thousands, maybe."

"Do you want me to try to find a home for them? I have pretty good luck helping horses." I wasn't sure I would have as much luck selling one as I did rescuing Dotty and Nickel, but I could give it a shot.

"Would you? Sure, that would be great," said Jeff. He sat back in his chair, watching me with smiling eyes. "There's something else you could do, if you wouldn't mind."

"What's that?" I would be happy to help him any way I could.

"See, I know you are the one that mostly takes care of the horses. You pick up my slack all the time for Daisy and Dancer."

"Glad you noticed."

"Hey, I didn't ask for them. I didn't ask for any of this mess and I'm just trying to do what I can to get my life started."

"I know, I know," I said. "You've been dealt a rotten set of cards. But you have friends who are glad to help you."

"I know and I appreciate it. So, do you think you could keep on picking up the slack for me? I mean, could you take over all the jobs with the horses, so I don't have to? So I can study and work and not worry about them? Except I can't pay you anything."

"I can do that. I do most of it anyway and I don't mind. I'd truly rather take care of them myself than worry that you're doing it wrong. You don't care much about horses, anyway, and I love them. I'm fine with that."

"They're big animals and I don't want to get run over."

"It's good that you respect their strength. When people don't, that's when they get hurt."

At that moment, my dad's green pickup with the mobile veterinary clinic on the back pulled into the yard. The mobile clinic is a fiberglass unit that fits in the bed of the pickup and has almost anything a vet might need, like water tanks, refrigerator, trays, and drawers to hold medicine and equipment. Dad parked next to Miss Julie's car, waved at us and got out.

"Hey, guys!" he said.

"Hi Dad." I was glad to have a distraction.

"Hi, Doc," said Jeff. "Where's your new partner?"

"Actually, he's at my house. I invited him for dinner and I'm on the way home. Thought I'd come by to see if my daughter was here and wanted a ride there." He looked at me with his eyebrows raised.

"You betcha," I said, glad to leave and go make some plans. How should a person go about selling a horse, anyway? We found Nickel from an index card at the clinic. Maybe that was the way to go.

"Jeff? Do you want to come for dinner, too? May as well make it a party." My dad liked Jeff a lot. Said he was a hard worker.

"No thanks, Doc," he said. "Miss J. is making her special meat loaf and I don't want to miss that."

"Okay, then. Tell her hi." Dad went back to his truck and started it up again.

"Well, I guess I've gotta go," I said. "See you." I turned and left the porch.

"Piper!" Jeff called. "We should talk about the horses some more—another time."

"We will. I have an idea. I'll catch up with you tomorrow."

I climbed in the truck and faced Dad, smelling medicine and horse manure.

"What is it, hon?" My dad can usually tell when I have an issue. That's not always a good thing, but today I was glad.

"You hired a new vet."

"Yes and…?"

"You never told me you were going to! I had to find out from everyone else."

"Did I need permission?"

"Well, no, but…jeez! You always tell me what's happening first."

Dad sighed. "Piper, I know. I know. But I had to find someone and this guy became available and I jumped on it. He seems like a really good fit. And anyway, it's not like I couldn't hire him without asking you. I'm glad you're so interested in the clinic, but sometimes things just need to get done. You know?"

"I guess." I was still annoyed at him, but Dad had a point. I didn't really have a voice in the running of the clinic. Maybe in the future I could, but I still wanted him to think of me as a responsible sort of junior partner.

Dad and I walked into his house and the tallest man I've ever seen rose from Dad's recliner.

"You said to come in and make myself at home, so I did. Hope you don't mind," said the man.

"Nope," said Dad. "Glad you did."

Red hair, a moustache, and a smiling face. I could see why Sue was attracted.

Dad introduced me to Eric Erickson. Was that a real name? We shook hands and sat down by the television while Dad pulled dinner together.

"So, Piper, what year are you in school?"

"I'm a sophomore."

"Oh, yeah? My daughter is a sophomore, too."

"Huh." What was I supposed to say?

"Your dad tells me you're a horsewoman."

"Well, my friend, Addie, and I have two horses that we share."

"Do you ride a lot?"

Honestly, it went on and on. I know he was trying to be polite, but not being very outgoing, I never know what to say to strange adults. Luckily, Dr. Erickson had an endless supply of questions.

"What classes are you taking?"

"Oh, the usual."

"Well, which one is your favorite?"

"I guess…English."

"You must like to read."

"Yeah, I do."

"That's good. How are your grades doing?"

"They're okay."

I was wiggling in my chair by the time he asked about my friends and what we liked to do after school, leaning in when he talked. His rotten breath nearly knocked me over, and besides, why was he being so nosy? Awkward.

"Dinner's ready!"

Hallelujah! At least Dad could talk to him while we ate.

Dad had prepared his Busy Day Guest Special: Caesar salad with broiled chicken breasts. I'm not crazy about it, but I was pretty hungry so I ate and didn't talk. The Serendipity Springs Veterinary Association (both of them) talked about farm calls, prices, clients and office procedures. I discovered that Dr. Erickson was looking for a house to rent and had been downsized from a five-man clinic in Louisville, due to the economy. Being from Minnesota originally, he loved ice hockey, but he also liked basketball, which I thought was a given for tall guys. He said he loved it here in Kentucky, because it was a basketball state.

After dinner, we all hung out in the family room, me, Dad and Doc Eric ("Oh, call me Doc Eric. You don't have to call me Dr. Erickson— we're friends now!") Dad and Doc Eric had beer, while I slurped my Coke down. I needed to be alone so I could call and check on Addie with no one to listen in.

"Piper, hello?" My dad and Doc Eric stared at me.

"What?"

"Eric just asked you a question. Where were you?"

"Oh, just…nothing. I'm sorry, what did you say?"

"I asked if you would meet my daughter and sort of show her around a little. Introduce her to all your friends." Dr. Eric stared at me with a smile.

Did he know I only had one friend? Well, maybe two, if you counted Jeff. But what could I say?

"Sure, okay. I can do that," I said.

"Great! She's coming here this weekend. Her mother has a three-month sabbatical coming up, so she'll be staying with me for the rest of the school year. I'm hoping she'll make some friends—it'll be easier getting used to a new place if she does."

"Yeah, sure."

I guess I didn't sound very enthusiastic, but I was thinking about Addie and wondering if she would want to hang out with the new girl.

I went to my bedroom as soon as I could after that and called Addie's phone. It rang and rang, but no answer. I texted:

HEY WHERE U AT?

I waited and waited. No response. What could she be doing?

Chapter Four

~ **Frenchy** ~

Addie never called me back and never texted me either. When I didn't hear and didn't hear, I got disgusted and quit trying. If she didn't want to talk to me, that was fine. I spent most of the rest of the weekend out at Miss Julie's, cleaning stalls and exercising the horses. They needed a lot of brushing, with their winter coats falling out. Horses look kinda moth-eaten if you don't get that old itchy hair brushed away. It flew off the brush, blew in my eyes and made me sneeze.

That Sunday afternoon, Jeff came out and actually helped with Daisy. He walked into the barn as I tied her to a ring on a post. After finding a brush, he stood on the far side of his horse and started to work.

"How's it going, Pipe? I know what we agreed on, but I have a little time today before Miss Julie needs me, so I can help. Easy, there." Daisy fidgeted nervously as a person she wasn't comfortable with touched her.

"Oh, you know…"

"When does the new veterinarian start at your dad's clinic?"

"Tomorrow, I think. He's renting a house in town for himself and his daughter. That's all I know."

"What's his name?"

"His name is Eric Erickson, but I'm supposed to call him Doc Eric. I don't know the daughter's name, but I've got to be her new buddy and

22

show her around. I'll bet she's tall, skinny, and redheaded."

"Huh."

"So, I haven't snapped at anyone today." I wanted to talk about what he said about me being crabby and was ready to continue our argument, defending myself.

"No." Jeff grabbed a currycomb and started on Daisy's tail. I stopped brushing and stood looking at him with my chin out and raised eyebrows, trying to get him to keep talking.

"Do you really want to do this now?" Jeff glared at me.

"I need to know why it bothers you so much when I say things that might be snappy, even if I don't mean to."

"Piper, look, I really like you. You're my best friend. You know me better than anyone. But when you snap at me like you do sometimes, it feels like back when my stepmom used to yell at me and cut me down. Cassie was a piece of work, remember?" Jeff shook his head and stared out the open barn door.

Now I felt awful. I knew his stepmom and how nuts she was. She literally never said anything nice to Jeff, although she was sweet as syrup to the rest of us. She was horrible to him. It was actually a good thing that she took off for South America, leaving the truck and horse for Jeff. We were all glad to see the last of her. But…I was his best friend? That was news, and I liked it, but I did not want to be compared to Cassie.

"I don't mean to snap," I said. "I was just so worried about the horses and it scared me thinking about what could have happened to them. But I don't want to sound like her, ever! I know how mean she was to you."

"So, still friends?" Jeff asking that made my heart break a little.

I remembered how sweet Jeff had been when we went to the Homecoming Dance. I wore a short dark blue dress—my first date and my first dance. It was a really fun night. Jeff was a pretty good dancer and Addie had taught me how to slow dance so I didn't embarrass myself. Dad drove us in his truck, which was awkward. We also walked to a movie once last January. Since then, Jeff took driving lessons and got his license, but that was it. Did he not want to go out with me anymore?

"Of course I'm your friend. And so is Addie. We're the Horse Rescuers, the three of us."

"Four, if you count Miss Julie."

"We have to count Miss Julie!"

"Well, okay then. And you're going to find someone to buy Daisy and Dancer? I feel like I'm putting too many of my responsibilities onto you, but I need to keep my grades up."

"Of course I will," I said, sounding more sure than I felt. "It will have to be a really nice person who will treat her well. She's a good girl." I rubbed Daisy's shining neck and she snorted her appreciation.

Jeff beamed as he put the brushes and currycomb back in the grooming box for me. I waited for him to say something else, but he didn't. I didn't know what else to say, so I led Daisy back to the paddock. The colt, Dancer, snorted and trotted around, waiting for his mom to come back. He was also a beautiful animal, and I hoped he would be worth some money, too. When I took her halter off, Daisy immediately walked in circles, then got down on her side and rolled in the dirt. Argh! They never failed to do that after you brushed them.

We walked up to the house together so I could say hi to Miss Julie. She sat at her kitchen table working on her laptop.

"Piper! How are you? Ready to go back to school?" Miss Julie was always the most upbeat person I knew.

"No way, no how!" I said. "What are you doing?"

"Oh, I'm working on my column for next week. I thought I'd introduce Dr. Erickson and tell a little bit about him. I'll need to go talk to him tomorrow. Did you like him?"

Miss Julie writes a column for the local county paper, The Serendipity Serenade. She writes about different individuals and what

24

they're doing.

"He was okay. Dad likes him, so they'll probably get along."

"Any more news about Addie and her … whatever he is? What is he, anyway? A crush, or is that word too out-of-date?" Miss Julie was rarely unable to find the right word. She used to be a teacher.

"I don't know—I can't get hold of her. I think he's just a guy she's hung up on."

"Let's hope she doesn't get too weird about him," put in Jeff. "Wisconsin is a long way away."

"Really," I agreed, not mentioning how old he was to either of them. Jeff was older than me by a couple years and I didn't want to make that seem a big deal.

After going home, I prepared an index card to put up in the clinic advertising a purebred Quarter Horse for sale. I had to leave parts blank because I didn't know how much money to ask for. I ended up spending the entire night watching movies and eating pizza with Mom until way too late. She'd been out with Sam Applegate earlier and was in a very romantic mood, so we saw two weepy chick flicks. I put Addie, Jeff and the new girl out of my mind and drifted off quickly.

Monday morning brought rain and more rain, typical spring weather. I was a sun-lover, never at my best when it was wet. That day was beyond soaking. You could have expected to see fish swimming down the street. All the kids at school were grumpy, not just me. After a week's break, to have to come back to school in the middle of a downpour was harsh. I found Addie by her locker and pulled her out of the hallway into an empty classroom.

"So why didn't you call me back—or at least send a text?" I asked.

"Piper, Duh! Dad took my phone away! I couldn't!"

"He what? Why?" Addie was hardly ever in trouble with her father. She was his baby girl and he saw her so rarely that she could pretty much get by with murder.

"Oh, it's so stupid! He checked my phone and found my texts to Joe. He found out how old Joe is and told me I couldn't see him anymore, *then* he took my phone and *then* he grounded me until I came back home!"

"Adds, what did your texts say?" I couldn't imagine my best friend saying anything too spicy in a text to a boy. Our parents had drilled into our heads how dumb that was, just asking for trouble.

"It wasn't what I said. It was what Joe said." Addie stood very still and looked at the ground.

"Which was…?"

"Oh, you know. Just stuff," she said.

"I don't know. Like what?"

"Hmm, things about kissing and stuff."

"Addie! Did you? Kiss…and stuff?"

"Well, yeah, I kissed him. No stuff though, I didn't want to." Addie had her arms crossed in front of her chest. "Are you done questioning me?"

"I wasn't…"

"You were! I know what you were thinking about me! Thanks a lot!" My best friend turned, grabbed a book out of a locker and stalked down the hallway. Which was suddenly empty. I would be late again for English.

I made it to class while Mr. Wieland was still checking attendance on his computer, so I snuck into a seat near the door. One or two of the kids waved at me, but mostly they stared at a girl sitting in the back row. Her clothes were gorgeous and so was she, with shiny auburn hair cut short, but pointy at the ears. She wore a brilliant blue suit like a TV anchorwoman would wear, blue heels (For school? Really?) and her nails were polished a shiny fuchsia. Bright lipstick that matched her nails. This girl did not look like a high school kid. Who was she? A model? Someone to speak to the class? But she had a backpack hanging from her chair like a student and she was writing in a notebook.

It crossed my mind that it might be Doc Eric's daughter, but I quickly scrapped that idea. No veterinarian would have such a fashionista kid. Vets and their families were more practical; I was sure of it. I heard someone behind me ask her where she was from and she whispered "Paree" very Frenchly. Thick accent. So she was from Paris! Surely it was Paris, France, and not Paris, Kentucky!

She didn't say a word during the rest of class, so I forgot about her until we all got up to leave. Frenchy stood, towering above the rest of the class, and slunk to the door. Honest, she slunk. Her hips moved independently from her body. Her silk blouse strained across the front of her chest—she was what the guys called "stacked".

As Frenchy walked down the hall, checking her class list, I noticed every boy she passed turning his head to watch. Wow, we had a babe at our school. Kimmy Smith, the class flirt and beauty queen would be jealous.

Addie and I always met after school and walked home together, so I sat on the steps outside and waited for her. Addie would come unless she was hugely mad. I watched everyone coming out, still looking for someone that might be Doc Eric's kid. The overhang of the roof kept me dry and as I sat, the rain slowed and stopped. After about fifteen minutes, I was just about ready to leave when Addie clunked down a heavy backpack next to me.

"I am done with boys forever!" she said, just like we had never argued.

"Now what?"

"Have you seen that new girl? The French one? Kimmy Smith says she heard her making a date with a senior!"

"She's pretty glitzy," I said, "but Kimmy Smith makes up things a lot."

"Yeah, so glitzy that's all the guys can think about. I heard them talking—gross!"

"So what?" I couldn't see how that affected us. "They're mostly geeks anyway." We had agreed on that at the beginning of the year.

"Yeah, but how can we compete with that?"

"We don't have to compete. We don't like those guys and we don't care what they think. Remember?"

"Well, yeah…" Addie was always torn between thinking guys were stupid and wanting to flirt with them and get their attention. I wasn't torn—most of them were stupid. Except for Jeff, who had his moments.

We walked to the Dairy Dog and got Slushy Sloshes to celebrate the rain stopping, raspberry for me, and cherry for Addie. She wanted to gossip some more about the French girl, but I had heard enough. Let the guys drool over her. I just hoped Jeff wouldn't see her—I didn't need that kind of competition.

Chapter Five

~ Jackie ~

Addie had to go home and face her mother about her dad and the texting issue. She wanted me to come with her, so her mother wouldn't yell, but I needed to stop by the clinic. We said goodbye and I walked to the clinic by myself. No cars at all except for Sue's minivan; no Dad and no clients.

Sue helped me clear a space on the bulletin board. The card that I pinned up read:

PUREBRED QUARTER HORSE MARE
BAY WITH WHITE STOCKINGS, 8 YRS. OLD
COLT AT SIDE
FOR SALE TO A GOOD HOME
BEST OFFER
LEAVE MESSAGE AT DESK

I crossed my fingers and went home, hoping that little ad would sell those horses and make Jeff really happy with me.

The rest of the week went pretty normal. Mom was still in her reorganizing phase and starting to sort through my closet. I wasn't about to let her do that without me there to supervise. We spent an entire evening going through my stuff. I saved some clothes from getting tossed and also got rid of a few things I had always hated. Mom had this image of me as a girly-girl, and wouldn't let go of it. She was thrilled that I wore a dress and went on a date last fall and again in the winter. I hoped she was learning that I mostly ran around in jeans and tee shirts, and that she would forget pink fluffy sweaters.

Addie got her mother to give back the phone and let her go out again, at least with me. Since we had not been anywhere together for a while, she talked me into a new scary movie at the theater in town. Addie loved Scream at Me, but it reminded me why I don't like scary movies. I've had some terrifying things happen to me in my life, like being attacked by Ugly Jake and being tied up and almost burnt in Miss Julie's basement. I don't like the fake scariness of horror movies. I spent some time out at the farm with the horses, but never saw Jeff. I knew he was studying and running errands for Miss Julie. It was nice that she found someone who could carry groceries and stuff for her, but it was extra nice for Jeff to have a place that felt like a home.

On Friday afternoon, I walked into the pasture and smiled at the sun. Apple trees bloomed, more flowers shot up every day, and the grass grew thick and green. The horses probably liked it more than I did. They gobbled up the juicy new growth and rolled in the sunshine. When I looked at my little herd, I always sent up a silent "Thank you," for them. I would be sad when Daisy and Dancer left, but I'd make sure they went to good homes. Jeff had mowed Miss Julie's grass for the first time, and the aroma drifted over to the horse paddock. It was my favorite smell, next to a warm horse.

A white pickup truck I didn't recognize pulled into the barnyard. Doc Eric got out and walked over to the fence, looking at my horses. I walked over to him and smiled to be polite, wondering what he wanted.

"Hello, Piper," he said with big smile.

"Hi," I said, bending my neck way back to see his face. "What's up?"

"I brought my daughter Jacqueline out to meet you. You are in the same class in school, I think."

He turned to the truck and motioned impatiently. The passenger door opened and someone got out. Coming around the side of the truck, she slunk toward us. Frenchy. Today, she wore a pale pink pants suit with matching heels. I stared.

Frenchy stepped over to the fence where Doc Eric and I stood, avoiding mud puddles and horse apples.

"Piper, this is my daughter, Jacqueline. Jacqueline, this is Piper, Dr. Jones' daughter. Piper is a horsewoman and takes care of these horses."

"Are they yours," the overdressed female asked, tottering over to us. Her English was good, even though her French accent was strong, but she said it in a flat, uninterested way. A snob? All the kids said she was.

"Well, the spotted pony and the grey gelding are mine and my friend, Addie's. We share them. Long story. The bay mare and foal belong to Jeff—he lives here with Miss Julie. It's her farm." I had decided not to get into a long story about Jeff and how he came to own the two horses and live on the farm.

"Jacqueline loves horses. Maybe you could take her for a ride sometime." Doc Eric was full of ideas, just not good ones.

"Sure, sometime," I said. Polite, but vague. That was the way I always got out of promising things.

"When?" Doc Eric persisted. "Today?" Jacqueline stared at me with large, brown, heavily made-up eyes. What was she thinking about his pushiness?

"Well, you can't ride in that," I said, pointing to her pantsuit. "You'll need some jeans." I could just picture her in the saddle in that. It would be a disaster to try to ride in tight pants and high heels.

Jacqueline looked at her father, with a tight lips and a red face. Doc Eric said, "I guess you'll have to go shopping. Again. Can't believe you need more clothes after what your mother bought you in New York." He paused. "How about tomorrow, then?"

Realizing he was talking to me, now, I shrugged.

31

"Tomorrow? Would that be a good time?"

I nodded, not able to think of an excuse.

"Around 10:00?"

I nodded again. What else could I have said? My mother's politeness lessons held a firm grip on me.

"Great!" said Doc Eric, "Let's go, sweetheart. Time to get some riding clothes."

Jacqueline immediately turned with her head down and climbed back into the truck. Her heels left tiny holes in the mud where they dug in. Her dad waved and drove off down the driveway faster than even my dad.

As I walked into the barn, I noticed Jeff standing in the yard. He had stopped the lawnmower and was watching the white truck driving away, his mouth open. I began cleaning out the dusty, plastic medicine cabinet. He wandered in to find me as I worked.

"Whoa! Who was that?"

"That was Dad's new partner, Doc Erickson and his daughter, Jacqueline." I gave it a heavy French pronunciation, *Jhzah-cleen*. "She's the one I'm supposed to become best buds with."

"Ah, she doesn't really look like your type."

"Not really and I have to go *riding* with her tomorrow. Can't wait."

"I hope she has other clothes for riding," said Jeff.

"Yeah, well she's gonna get Daddy to buy her some jeans. But maybe she'll show up in an English riding habit."

"Maybe she's not so bad," he said.

"Or maybe she's worse," I said. She would look spectacular in jeans and maybe Jeff would start drooling. Maybe he was already drooling.

Saturday morning dawned clear and bright. The sun shone, birds

32

sang, but my heart was dragging on the ground with my feet. I walked slowly all the way out to the farm. I loved to ride my horses, it was my favorite thing, but it turned out to be a chore when I had to do it with someone I didn't even know.

Miss Julie knelt on the ground, planting pansies in the bed around her front porch. Honey sat in the grass nearby panting with a doggie grin on her face. Willie Nelson purred in a sunbeam on the steps. It was a happy picture of spring, but one I couldn't enjoy.

"Piper! Good morning! Don't you just love spring?"

"Hi, Miss Julie. Usually I do."

"But not today? Whatever is wrong?" With an effort and a grimace, Miss Julie got to her feet and sat down on the step beside Willie Nelson. Her bright blue eyes peered at me.

"I have to take Doc Erickson's daughter riding and I don't know if I even like her." Miss Julie had a way of making you tell the truth.

"Why not?"

"She's too fancy and she's stuck up." As I said it, I wondered if it was actually true.

"Oh, my!" said Miss Julie. "How do you know that?"

"Just the way she dresses at school. And she won't talk to anyone. All the kids think she's a snob," I said. A white pickup came down the lane.

"Well, this must be her. Give her a chance, why don't you? I'm going to interview her father for the paper. Bring her in after your ride and introduce us." Miss Julie headed inside where she would probably make iced tea or lemonade and pull out her famous cookies.

I walked over to the pickup truck and stopped, waiting for my riding companion to get out. Jacqueline climbed out and stood in front of me in a brand-new pair of jeans and a pink sweatshirt with a white kitten on it. At least she wore sneakers and today didn't have a lot of makeup on.

"Are these clothes agreeable to you?" she wanted to know.

"Oh, sure," I said, thinking the kitten sweatshirt looked like one that a woman Miss Julie's age would wear. But I had been right about the jeans. They fit her like a second skin, showing all her curves. "Let's go find the horses."

"Jacqueline, I'll be here talking to Mrs. Applegate," called Doc Eric from the truck.

"All right, Papa." She gave me a little smile and followed me into the barn. Doc Eric walked up to the house for his interview with Miss Julie, and we were alone.

Not knowing how to chat with her, I collected two halters and stalked out to catch the horses we would ride. Nickel was easy, as always. I led him in and tied him to a post in the barn. Dotty was a little harder to catch, leading me around the pasture for a few minutes before she gave in and allowed me to put the halter on her sleek, spotted head. There was nothing for Jacqueline to do, so she pretty much just stood around while I got the horses.

"Which one am I to ride?" asked Jacqueline.

"You should ride this grey one," I said, pointing to Nickel. I had considered putting her on Dotty so she would get bucked off, but then if she got hurt, I would be in trouble. Besides, that would be mean and I didn't want to be a mean person.

"Grey? He looks white, with some freckles."

"Well, you always call white horses greys—even if they look white—unless they are albinos with pink eyes and noses."

"You know much about horses. This one is very tall," she said, eyeing the saddle I was putting on his back.

"Have you ridden before?"

"Horse riding is not something I have done much. But a little in France."

"Did you ride English or Western in France?"

"We had a smaller, flat saddle. Not like this one." She pointed to

Nickel's beautiful hand-tooled Western saddle that Dad had given me for Christmas.

"That's a Western saddle. So how come you are French and your dad is not?"

"Well, I have grown up in Paris with my mother. She and my papa are not...I don't know how to say it. They do not live together?"

"Oh, okay. So then you came here to visit your dad?"

"Oui, yes. My mama had to go to Italy for three months. She wanted me to get to know my papa, so they arranged for me to come here to visit and go to school."

"How do you like it, so far?"

Jacqueline gave a big sigh. "The weather is nice, school is not hard, but..." she shrugged.

"But what?"

Jacqueline looked me in the eyes. "The other students do not seem friendly and my papa is, um, too careful with what I can do?"

"Overprotective?"

"Yes! What a wonderful word! He is overprotective. He only wants me to be friends with people who are safe; he only wants me to go places he approves. It is tiring." She rolled her eyes and I began to like her. Maybe she wasn't so bad after all.

"I can imagine. Mine is the same way sometimes. Are you ready to ride?"

"I think so," Jacqueline said, doubtfully, looking worried.

"Nickel is a sweetie. He'll take care of you. He's blind in one eye, but he will go very smoothly and not jump around. He's not that tall. He just looks like it next to her." I pointed to Dotty. "She bucks a little, so I don't think you should start out on her."

"Oh. What is that other horse? With the baby? She is beautiful."

I explained about how Daisy was a purebred Quarter Horse and how they were bred for cowboys to ride.

"The cowboys in the West?" So I explained how Quarter Horses were called that because they were the fastest horses there were for a quarter of a mile. They were faster even than thoroughbreds for a short distance. I went on to explain how POA ponies were bred down from Appaloosa horses, and that Arabian horses were from the deserts of the Middle East. I thought I had done a good job of explaining my collection of horses, where they were all from, and how they came to be developed, but she didn't seem to care at all about that. Jacqueline had another question.

"But the Quarter Horses are from the West? Like the saddles?"

"Yes, Jacqueline. From the West. You can climb on now."

"So American!" she said. She stared at Daisy and Dancer, even as she swung up onto Nickel's back. "That one is beautiful," she said, pointing at Daisy.

"She is, but let's just ride, Jacqueline," I said, mounting Dotty.

She laughed for the first time. "Please, Piper, call me Jackie. All my friends at home call me that. Only Papa calls me Jacqueline." This girl wasn't so bad, and she liked horses, which was a big plus.

The ride actually went fine. We walked down the path behind the barn and followed it over a hill and through some woods. We passed an old shack and I explained how Addie and I kept Dotty when we rescued her from Ugly Jake, her owner. It had turned out that Dotty was Miss Julie's old pony. It was a long story, but in the end, Dotty was mine and Addie's forever. She was a sweet horse, and I patted her shoulder, remembering. Jackie was amazed that we had been so bold as to rescue her and then Nickel.

We must have ridden for an hour then headed home. I jumped off Dotty. Jacqueline climbed down from Nickel and helped me brush them both. We let them out into their paddock and walked to the house, where Doc Eric and Miss Julie waited on the porch. Doc introduced his daughter to Miss Julie.

"How was your ride?" asked Miss Julie.

"Oh, fine," I said.

"Jacqueline?" prompted Doc Eric. Jackie's gaze met mine and we smiled at each other.

"The horse riding was very nice. Thank you so much, Piper. It was fun."

"Piper, I was looking at that Quarter Horse mare you have there." Doc Eric stared at the paddock and horses.

"Yeah, but she's not mine, she's Jeff's. She's pretty, isn't she?"

"Oh, I see. Yes, she's beautiful. Has she been his long?"

"Only since last fall, why?"

"Well, she looks like a mare I knew when I worked in Louisville."

"She did come from Louisville. Her name is Daisy and she has papers."

"Yes, it seems to be the same horse. I'd like to look at the papers sometime."

"Why?"

"The horse I knew was prone to colic. I'll ask my old clinic for the information. Your friend Jeff needs to know that if it's his horse."

"Wow! I'll tell him. Thanks," I said, wondering how to tell Jeff that his horse might get sick.

"Oh, well, sure, you're welcome. Thank you from me, also, Piper. Maybe you can ride together again soon. Thanks for the iced tea, Miss Julie." Doc Eric stood and walked down the steps.

"Thank you! The article about you should be out on Thursday. I'll be sure to get you a few copies." Miss Julie waved goodbye.

"Okay, 'bye now!" The two walked to the truck, got in and sped up the lane.

"What a very quiet girl," said Miss Julie.

"I know. She doesn't talk much. I think she's not at home speaking English, but she loves horses."

"And she's stunning."

"Yes, she is," I said, strangely wishing that Jeff would not see her again.

"I wonder if she feels weird here—it's definitely not like France." Miss Julie always looked for reasons for people's faults. "I hope you'll make her feel comfortable. I'll bet she's lonely."

"Well, I think you may be right. The kids at school aren't being friendly. Where's Jeff?"

"He drove the truck to pick up some feed. Your dad called and said he wouldn't have time to get it today."

No Jeff, Addie at swimming lessons. What was there for me to do? Homework? Nah, it was Saturday morning still. I went home, found a good book and sat in the porch swing trying to read. Instead, my mind kept wandering. Was Jackie going to be my friend? Would Jeff think she was stunning, too? I was glad he wasn't there to see her in her jeans and stare again. Could I still be friends with her if he did?

Chapter Six

~ Green Eyes ~

Sunday morning was rainy again, so I went over to Addie's house. We sat in her purple-on-purple bedroom and tried to solve all the problems of the world. The main ones, as we saw it, were: What Should Addie Do About Joe? How Does Jeff Feel About Piper? How Do We Feel About Jackie? How Can Piper Sell Jeff's Horses?

I had told Addie about trying to sell the horses and she agreed that it was nice of me and might make Jeff like me more. She thought the index cards were a good start, but I might want to try Craigslist. I thought that sounded like a big hassle. I didn't tell her about the possible colic, because I hoped that wasn't true or wouldn't make a difference.

It was impossible to ride with the heavy rain, so we watched a chick flick and baked a frozen pizza.

On Monday, I went to school as usual. Going to English class, I bumped into Jackie, who beamed at me. She was pretty anyway, but when she smiled, it was like the sun coming out.

"Piper!" she said. "I have something to tell you." Kids in class turned to look at us.

"Yeah? Tell me after class. Mr. Wieland is on a rampage today."

When class was over, she followed me as I headed for my locker, where Addie was waiting for me.

"Piper! I want to tell you what I have decided!" She looked at me, then Addie. "Hello, Addie."

"Hi, Jacqueline," said Addie.

Kimmy Smith stood by a water fountain two classrooms away, watching. Now what was she doing? Usually she hung out where there were lots of boys.

"Please, you must call me Jackie. My friends back home call me Jackie. No one says Jacqueline except my father and my teachers."

"Okay, Jackie." Addie smiled at her, really smiled.

"What did you want to tell me?" I asked.

"I have decided I want a horse!"

"What?" Addie and I said in unison. She wanted a horse. She's been here less than a week, and she wants a horse? Addie and I had waited years to get a horse and then we had to plot and scheme to rescue Dotty. A lot of planning went into getting Nickel, too. Was her overprotective dad also a pushover for whatever Jackie wanted? Would Jackie get a horse with a snap of her fingers? It didn't seem fair.

"Yes! Isn't it wonderful?" Jackie beamed.

"Yeah, sure, that's great," I said. Jackie getting a horse would mean she'd be out at the farm a lot. Where Jeff could see her. Did I want that? No! All of a sudden, I felt funny about Jackie. I didn't want her beautiful self out at the farm every day. I needed to get away and think.

"Jeez! Look at the time! Gotta go—see ya, Jackie!" I hustled down the hallway with Addie in tow.

"What was that about?" panted Addie, catching her breath.

"Do you think I want her out at the farm every day, wanting to ride? And…and getting to be friends with Jeff? Hanging out with him?"

"You're jealous!"

"No, I'm not. I just don't want to take any chances." Adds had to be wrong. I couldn't be a jealous person. I was a nice person.

"What chances?" Addie could be such a pain when she didn't see things my way.

"Hello, girls," crooned a sultry voice. A wave of perfume drifted over us as Kimmy Smith wiggled her blonde self up beside us. "I didn't know you were buds with the French Poodle." She snickered and raised her eyebrows.

"Who?" I asked.

"That one. Jacqueline. She asked me when the Pep Club meeting was. I told her the wrong night." Kimmy doubled over as if she were the funniest person in the world. "She'll get there and there won't be anybody there. It will be great! Serve her right for flirting with our guys. Don't be friends with her, you all—she's a loser. Gotta go, my posse is waiting!" Kimmy arched her neck in a "Look at me" posture and sashayed down the hall.

Addie and I stared at the rear end of her.

"Wow! She's as mean as ever," said Addie. "We should tell Jackie about the meeting."

"You can if you want to. I wonder if Jackie *has* been flirting," I said, ready to believe the worst.

"Remember what we used to call Kimmy back in junior high? Kimmy the Snake. No one could ever trust her to tell the truth and she always tried to get us in trouble."

"Well, I just wonder. Hey, are you going out to the clinic with me after school? I have to see if anyone called about Daisy."

"Nah, I have swimming again. See ya!"

When school was out, I walked to the clinic and checked the bulletin board. The card was gone, but no one had called. Maybe it would happen soon. I let Sue know about it and told her to be sure to call me if anyone asked about Daisy. What more could I do?

I poked my nose into Dad's office while he was talking on the phone. Sitting down in a chair, I waited for him to be done with his call.

"What's up, buttercup?" he said after he was done.

"I promised Jeff I'd help him sell Daisy. He needs the money and is so busy getting A's and applying for scholarships that he doesn't have the time."

"I've talked to him about college. I think he's got a pretty good shot at a full scholarship if his grades are good. He's definitely decided to sell the horses, then?" Dad toyed with the stethoscope in his lab coat pocket.

"Yeah, he's never been into horses. That was his stepmom's thing, and she was nuts. Daisy deserves an owner who loves her, and I'm trying to find one for them both. Dancer's old enough to separate from his mother, though, isn't he? If we have to?"

"Sure he is. We just don't have enough pasture to do it at Julie's. Those two should be worth a good bit."

"Like...how much?"

"Well, you never know, and prices for horses go up and down, but possibly thousands."

"Wow! And someone took the card I left here. If that doesn't work out, what should I do next?"

"You could try calling some Quarter Horse breeders. There are some around here and she's a beautiful mare with a healthy foal. Really good bloodlines."

"Okay, I'll start checking around. Can you give me some names?"

"There are only two that I go to regularly. I'll check with them and see if you can call them. But why don't you go online, too? See if there is anyone else local that might be interested."

"Okay, Dad. It's a plan." I smiled with relief that I knew what I was going to do next. I hugged my dad and went home.

I waited three days, but didn't hear from Sue about the index card.

Deciding that maybe the person had changed their mind, I made five more cards to put on the bulletin board. They said:

BEAUTIFUL PUREBRED QUARTER HORSE MARE AND COLT
AT SIDE
MARE IS BAY WITH WHITE STOCKINGS, 8 YRS. OLD
FOR SALE TO A GOOD HOME
BEST OFFER
CALL PIPER: 555-634-5789

I figured if I gave my cell phone number, I wouldn't have to check with Sue every day. I put all five cards on one pin and stuck them to the bulletin board. There seemed to be lots of other horse ads, but none for Quarter Horses, so I kept my hopes up.

When I got home I went online, but couldn't find any local breeders besides the ones Dad had given me. I found out that some horses were worth as much as $10,000, more if they had good bloodlines and training. That was fantastic and I couldn't wait to tell Jeff.

On Friday, when I got to school, Addie lurked by my locker. She pounced on me as I walked up.

"Pipe, did you hear what happened?"

"No, what?"

"Two junior boys got in a fight and got sent home."

"Already?" It wasn't even 8:00 am yet.

"Yes, and guess what they were fighting about? Jackie!"

"No way! So she *has* been making trouble." I threw my stuff in my locker and grabbed my English book and notebook. I scurried off to class, waving goodbye to Addie. I would see if Jackie was in class today.

And she was. She looked across two rows of desks at me with large, sad eyes, like she wanted me to do something. I felt kinda bad for her, but what was I supposed to do? If she got the boys all crazy, it was her problem to deal with. Did I want to get in the middle of that? No! What if she got Jeff all worked up and nuts over her? I didn't want to take her side.

Mr. Wieland kept asking questions, so I couldn't turn around to see Jackie. I had to look down so as not to get called on—a habit of mine. When class was over, she started to come toward me, but I hurried out and hid in the girl's bathroom till it was safe to go to my next class. Talk about feeling guilty, but I didn't know how I felt about her! I avoided her so I didn't have to think about it.

It was exhausting, hiding from Jackie all day. I spent my precious lunchtime in the library, and all afternoon sneaking around the halls. When Addie and I met up after school, she had more information.

"Piper, did you know Jackie got sent to the principal's office, too? Madison told me in study hall." Aha! That was why she had looked so weird. Getting sent to the office your first week of school was a bad thing.

"Because of the fight, right?"

"Gotta be. I wonder what really happened? Have you talked to her?"

"Adds, you know the fight was over her. She must have gotten both guys all worked up, so they each thought they were her boyfriend. And no, I haven't talked to her."

"We should ask her."

"I don't want to. Come and check the want ads with me at the clinic." I felt mean, but tried not to think about it anymore.

We wandered over to Serendipity Vet Clinic. We walked in the front door, since there were no client cars parked in front, for once. Looking at the bulletin board, I couldn't believe it: all the cards had been taken.

"Hi, Piper! Hi, Addie!" Sue came out from the back with some folders in her hand.

"All the cards are gone! Yay, there must be lots of people interested in the horses!" This was such great news, I grabbed Addie's arm and squeezed. "Can't wait! I hope they call soon!"

"Me, too," said Addie. "It'll be a weight off Jeff's mind, and you can quit obsessing over it."

Sue turned as someone from the back of the clinic called her name. She was gone for a moment and came back, without the files, and holding a coffee mug.

"I met Eric's daughter, Jackie, a while ago. Nice kid," she said. "Isn't she in your class at school?"

"She was here?" I asked. "At the clinic?" I couldn't get away from her.

"Yeah, she walked here from school to ride on a farm call with her dad. They left just before you got here."

Oh, jeez! She was taking over all the places in my life, and I still couldn't decide how I felt about her. I explained all that to Addie as we left the building, but she was so busy trying to text Joe in Wisconsin that she didn't really hear me. I finally stopped walking and stood in front of her until she put down the phone.

"Adds, are you listening?"

"Well, sure I am."

"Then what did I say?"

"Oh, something about the clinic, the farm and school and all the places you love."

"No! I *said* that Jackie is showing up in all the places I love. Next she'll be in my mom's or my dad's house and in my bedrooms there. She's taking over my whole world."

"Well, Pipe, her dad works with your dad at the clinic. She's got to go to school and she only rode the horse that one time. Get over it."

"She wants her own horse, remember? She'll be everywhere! Even in Miss Julie's house!"

"Aha! That proves it. You're afraid Jeff will like her. You're jealous because she's so pretty." Addie started laughing. "The green-eyed monster has got you!"

"Of course not. Don't be stupid."

"You are! You're afraid Jeff will fall for her and she'll even take over your boyfriend. Maybe she even likes blues and science fiction." Addie knew all about Jeff's musical and literary tastes.

"Addie, shut up! He's not my boyfriend and he can do what he wants. If he wants her, he's welcome to her."

"Does he know he's not your boyfriend?"

"What do you mean?" I stared at my best friend. She could really pinpoint problems. I actually didn't know what Jeff thought about me, not really. I knew we were friends, but beyond that, who knew? I sure didn't.

"I just think you should think about it, Piper." Addie looked in my eyes. "Jeff is crazy about you. You're making up problems, when maybe there really aren't any."

Addie waved goodbye and started off in the direction of her house, still texting. I hoped she wouldn't walk into a tree, and God help her when she started driving. As I crossed the street heading home, I stopped right on the centerline, saying, "Holy cow!" Addie was right again. I was jealous. A horn honked at me and I hurried to the far sidewalk.

Was she right about all of it? Was Jeff really crazy about me? Was I making up problems? I didn't think so, but I hardly ever thought I was wrong and Addie had a long track record of being right about these things. I thought about it as I walked home to dinner. There was a note on the refrigerator where Mom and I left notes for each other. It said: GONE TO DINNER WITH SAM. PIZZA IN FREEZER.

Ugh. I hated the idea of another frozen pizza, so I pulled out my phone and called Dad.

"Piper?"

"Hi, Dad, what's for dinner at your house?"

"Oh, well, I'm cooking burgers—want to come over?"

"Yeah, Mom went out and there's only frozen pizza here. I'll be over in a couple of minutes."

"Okay, honey."

"Fine, see you."

I showed up at Dad's house ten minutes later pretty hungry. Even if dinner wasn't ready, I can always rely on him to have a lot of good snacks, especially with Eric coming over. I walked in the front door, yelled "Hello!" and looked in the kitchen.

Sitting there at the table were Doc Eric...and Jackie.

Chapter Seven

~ The Vindicators ~

Doc Eric was drinking iced tea with lemon, since he was evidently on call, and Jackie had a Coke in her hand. She looked at me with troubled eyes, sitting in my father's house.

"Piper, hello!" said Dad's new partner. "Honey, say hello to Piper."

"Hello, Piper," said Jackie, watching me. What was going on with her, anyway? Why was she staring like that?

"Sweetie," said Dad, "did I tell you Jackie was coming, too?"

"Not so much. Hi, Jackie," I said, wondering if I could escape and feeling incredibly guilty, I looked around, but couldn't think of a reasonable excuse. I decided I'd just have to tough it out and try to leave early. Luckily, it was my night to sleep at Mom's house, so I wouldn't have to stay here all night, waiting for them to leave.

The evening turned into a difficult one anyway. Doc Eric tried to get Jackie and me to talk about school. He asked question after question about what we were taking, who were our teachers, who we hung out with. He even pried into my social life, asking if I was dating yet. Jackie tried to answer everything, but left out the part about going to the principal's office. She seemed embarrassed and I would have been, too. But I didn't even try to be friendly. I was every parent's image of a grouchy, uncommunicative teenager. I wasn't proud to be acting that way, but I didn't know how to act when I was jealous of someone. I

48

wanted to be a good person, but what if she wanted a boyfriend, and it turned out she wanted Jeff?

Dad was busy in the kitchen during Jackie's and my inquisition by Doc Eric. Once he served the burgers, things got a little better because he and Doc Eric talked about medical issues. Jackie and I didn't talk, but her face grew redder as the evening progressed and she wouldn't look at me. I got busy cleaning up and left as early as I possibly could, excusing myself with lies about homework. After I got home, I crawled into bed to read, glad Mom was still out with Sam. I didn't want to have to explain myself.

When my phone rang, the blues riff told me it was Jeff.

"Hi, Jeff."

"Hi, Piper. What're you doing?"

"Reading in bed. Nothing much. What are you doing?"

"I've been writing an essay and had to stop. I'm too tired. I've had it."

"You're working tonight?"

"Gotta do it, Pipe. If I get a scholarship, maybe I can relax."

"Well, let's hope so!"

"So, have you gotten anywhere with selling the horses?"

"I will. Don't worry—they'll sell real soon, I know it." I sounded more sure than I really was. "By the way, do you have the papers for Daisy?"

"Yeah, I think they're in the big file I got out of Cassie's room." Cassie was his lunatic stepmother that left him the horse and truck when she went to South America. "Do you need them?"

"I want to check and make sure they're in order before we sell Daisy and Dancer. All six index cards have disappeared, which means people are interested. That's a good sign. Hey, guess what? I looked up Quarter Horses for sale online and some can go for $10,000!"

"You're kidding!"

"No, really. We have to check the papers you have and see what their bloodlines are. Some are crazy expensive, and Dad says Daisy's lines are good."

"Wow, thanks. Just let me know, will you?"

"You bet. I feel good about it."

"Okay, um, hey Piper? Do you want to go to a movie tomorrow night?"

"I guess. Where?" My heart pounded. Yes!!

"There's one I want to see playing at the Moxie in town. The Vindicators 2."

"Yeah, I'll go. That's supposed to be good. What time?"

"I'll come get you at 7:30, okay?"

"Sounds good." I smiled to myself. It sounded great!

"Yeah, see you then."

"'Bye."

So then of course I had to text Addie and tell her what I was doing the next night. She texted back immediately.

ALL RIGHT PIPER! GO GIRL! HAVE FUN HAHA SEE YA LATER. ;-)

On Friday morning, I was getting ready for school when Dad called, as I expected. I had my attitude ready.

"Piper, what was going on last night?"

"I don't know."

"You do know and I wish you'd tell me. I've never seen you be so rude."

"Dad, I didn't mean to be rude, but I just didn't have anything to say."

"Well, you could have tried. Eric and Jackie are nice people, and you aren't even giving them a chance."

"Jeez, Dad, sorreee! What do you want me to say?"

"Say you'll be nicer next time."

"Okay, okay, I'll be nicer. Dad? I'm going to a movie with Jeff tonight."

"Where, Piper?"

"Just the Moxie."

"Okay. What is your curfew time?"

"Mom lets me stay out till 11:00 on Friday nights."

"Well, have fun and be home on time."

"Yes, Daddy Dear."

"You know I mean it."

"Dad, all right!"

"Okay, then. I love you. 'Bye!"

"'Bye, Dad."

After that, I was happy to eat some crunchy granola cereal and hustle off to school. The day dragged, but I was still feeling weird about Jackie, so I avoided her. After class I didn't see Addie anywhere, so I hurried home to sort through my clothes. I had to find something to wear that night that was flattering.

My mother danced in circles that I actually had another date. She giggled and helped me pick out a shirt to wear. It was turquoise and soft, not something I wore a lot, but I loved it because it was so comfortable. Mom said it made me look adorable, which sounded odd, but I liked the feeling. I washed my hair and blew it dry so it was full and fluffy. When

Jeff came to the door, he said, "Wow!" which made it all worth it.

As I climbed into the seat of Jeff's truck, he said, "Piper, you look great."

"Thanks," I said. "Did you clean out your truck?"

"Yeah, I'm glad you noticed. I have to take it to the garage tomorrow to get the transmission checked out." Jeff pulled out of my driveway and drove slowly through town.

"What's wrong with it? It runs, doesn't it?"

"Sometimes it slips out of gear. I'm hoping I don't have to get a whole new transmission. It's big bucks to replace one."

"Like how much?"

"Thousands. It's always something with cars or trucks. I couldn't drive it much until I got insurance, and that set me back a bundle. Now there's something broken." Jeff was sounding more down than I'd ever heard him.

"That's tough." What else could I say? I took a deep breath and asked about something that had been bothering me. "Is that why you haven't asked me to go anywhere lately?"

Jeff looked over at me and laughed, but not a happy laugh. "Piper, it's not because I didn't want to. I couldn't drive the truck, I have zero money for movies and stuff, and I have to spend all my time studying or working to pay for the truck. I can pay for tonight because I'm working extra for Mr. Simpson tomorrow."

"Oh. Well, I could pay sometimes." The main words I had heard were that he actually had wanted to ask me out. Thrilled, but not knowing anything else to say, I threw a random fact out about the movie we were going to. "Josh Channing broke his wrist while he was filming this movie. He kept the cast on to finish the movie and they wrote it into the script."

"Cool. Most Hollywood types wouldn't finish if they got hurt, they'd just delay the film."

"I think some of them would. Look at John Massif and Sam Dudely. They're pretty tough."

"They aren't tough, they're just Hollywood pretty boys." Jeff grinned as he disagreed, knowing that we were in for a long argument. Jeff was so easy to be with it didn't matter if we agreed or not. He rarely argued so hard that he got upset.

"I don't think so," I said. "Both those guys live on ranches when they aren't making movies."

"And that makes them tough? Hah! They hire people to do the chores. Just because they have a ranch doesn't mean they work on it. They just like to say they have one. Makes 'em sound macho."

And so, the good-natured argument went on while we bought a large popcorn to share, sodas, and were choosing seats in the darkened theater.

"Piper, see that girl sitting in front?"

"The one with the denim shirt?"

"Yeah, is that your friend, Jackie?"

I looked hard. "Nah, she's taller and prettier than that."

"I guess you're right. She's definitely curvier and prettier." Wait, *what* did he say? And why was he looking for Jackie?

"So, Jeff, how pretty do you think she is?"

"Well, I'm not blind. She's gorgeous and..."

"And what?"

Jeff thought this was another fun argument, but I couldn't get past my jealousy.

"Oh, it doesn't matter." Sensing danger, Jeff began eating popcorn very fast.

"It does matter. Gorgeous and what?" My voice was louder than I wanted it to be. Jeff sighed and turned to me.

"Jackie is gorgeous. She has a great figure, all right?"

I drank my Coke and was silent.

"Piper? What?"

I drank and was silent.

"You can't be mad that I said that."

"Can too!"

"Why? It's the truth! You asked if I thought she was pretty. Do you want me to lie about it?"

"No!"

"Then what?"

"I just want... I don't know. I didn't know you thought she was so hot!"

"Everyone in school thinks she's hot."

"Well, you're not everyone." What was I, chopped liver? Couldn't he compliment me once, while he was raving about her?

"But I am human. And a guy. We look at girls, it's what we do."

"Well, have fun with that, Mr. Human Guy!" I handed him the popcorn. Okay, I pretty much threw it at him, folded my arms and sat back in my seat.

The movie came on then and we watched it in silence, Jeff eating popcorn and glancing at me every few minutes. I knew he was looking for a sign that I was over it, but I wasn't and couldn't pretend I was.

As we walked out of the Moxie an hour and a half later, I said, "I'll just walk home, Jeff."

"Oh, come on, Piper. I'll drive you. You can't still be mad."

"Look, I need to be by myself and think, okay?"

I figured it wouldn't take me long to walk home. Tears blinded me, but I knew the way and could have gotten home blindfolded. I ignored my ringing phone and kept stomping down the street. After about two blocks, a familiar blue Cougar rolled up beside me.

The Quarter Horse

"Do you want a ride?" said Miss Julie.

"Oh, I'm okay," I said, not wanting to talk about why I was crying.

"Come on, get in, Piper. I'm on my way home from my book club and I'm going right past your house." Miss Julie was very firm when she wanted to be, a habit from being a teacher all her life. I got in the car and we arrived at my house in just a few minutes. Miss Julie has always had a lead foot. Most people don't know how many speeding tickets she's avoided by being a cute little old lady, but I do.

As I opened the door to get out, she put a hand on my arm and said, "Piper, I know you think your life is terrible now, but some day you'll look back on this and laugh."

"Doubt that!" I retorted through my sniffles.

"Good night, honey," she said as I shut the car door and waved goodbye.

I slipped in the back door, trying to make it to my bedroom without being heard. My bed was soft and warm. Could I hide under my patchwork quilt for a few weeks? I stuck my head under my pillow and gave in to some built-up howls and sobs.

My brain continued spinning with unfair questions. How could he be so mean? Did he not care at all? Did he think she was prettier than I was? But also, how could I be so silly and immature? What was wrong with me?

I decided if he wanted her, he could have her. I was done with him. All men cared about were looks. So what if we connected in our heads? It didn't matter to him. He could have Jackie and good riddance to him!

Chapter Eight

~ We're All Crazy ~

I woke up Saturday morning with a headache. I think now it was the fairness part of my brain, waging war on the crabby unfair part. As I padded to the kitchen in my socks, looking for an aspirin, Mom sat at the table with a cup of coffee.

"So what happened last night, honey? I heard you come in early."

"Oh, nothing, really."

"Piper, you don't have to be secretive. Do you think I would be upset with you for having an argument with your boyfriend?"

"He's not my boyfriend. And how did you know we argued?"

"I heard you in your room. Why else would you come home early and cry? I wanted to let you get it out before I asked you about it. So what happened?" Mom was nothing if not persistent.

So I poured out the whole miserable story to her, even admitting that I threw the popcorn at Jeff and walked home after the movie.

"Wow, honey, you must have been really upset. How do you feel now?"

I considered. How did I feel?

"I just...I feel silly and dumb for acting like I did and ruining a Friday night. And my head hurts like crazy from crying. But Mom? I can't help being mad at him for thinking Jackie is sooooo pretty and sexy."

"But you asked him if he thought she was."

"Yes, but I didn't think he'd admit it! He called her gorgeous! Mom, why are you smiling? This isn't funny!"

"No, I know it's not funny. I'm smiling because believe it or not, I had the same argument with your father when we were dating, way back before we got married."

"You're right, I don't believe it. And Mom? Your marriage broke up. You didn't stay married."

"Well, no, but that's not the reason we got divorced. Let me ask you something. Do you think Sam is cute?"

"Duh, yeah! Sam is a first-class hunk. And I know what you're saying, Mom, but it's not the same thing. Sam is much older than I am. I can think he's good-looking and it doesn't threaten Jeff."

"Piper, just think about it, okay? And think about the fact that sometimes with girls, hormones make us feel emotions we don't want to. We get irrational. As you get older, you'll learn to deal with those feelings better."

"I hope."

So I ate a banana and checked my phone for messages. Addie had gone with her mother to see her Aunt Amy, after which she had swim class. There was one text from Jeff that said CAN WE TALK? I ignored it and rode my bike out to see the horses. I planned on the way that if Jeff was on the porch at Miss Julie's or if I saw him around anywhere, I would make a U-turn and ride back home. I didn't want to face him. I wasn't ready to talk. Was I angry or embarrassed? I didn't know and that was a problem.

His truck was gone, so I was safe. He was probably at the garage with it. As always, being outside with the horses calmed me. I spent a restful hour in the barn, brushing each one and rubbing their faces and necks. Nickel especially seemed to know I was sad. He pushed his nose into my hair and nibbled, snorting. I hugged his neck, smelled warm horse, and sighed.

A gentle breeze blew in from the field outside and I heard Miss Julie calling her dog. I let the horses back into their paddock and wandered up to the house where Miss Julie swept the big wooden porch.

"Hello, Piper!"

"Hi, Miss Julie," I said.

"How are you today?"

"I'm okay. Did Jeff say anything?"

"No, but I could tell he was upset. He's usually cheerful, but today he was really quiet. Can I help?"

"Maybe. I don't know if I can put it into words."

"All right, sweetie. Let me know if I can do anything. By the way, Jeff will be gone all day. He took his truck to the garage and then had a large cleaning job to do for Mr. Simpson at school." A nice thing about Miss Julie was she would back off if you weren't ready to talk. Another was she seemed to know what was important and when. I relaxed for the first time all morning.

Honey had come wiggling up to me, wanting me to throw the soft, little Frisbee she loved. I skimmed it across the yard and the little golden sheltie ran after it. She grabbed it in her jaws and trotted back, panting, with the pink and green disk hanging off one tooth. She looked so funny, Miss Julie and I both laughed.

I threw it again farther. It landed in the lilac bushes and Honey had to search for it. As she searched, the half-grown kitten rubbed on my side, purring. Life was so sweet out here at the farm with all the animals. Why couldn't everything always be so uncomplicated?

I lay on my back and stared at the pale blue porch ceiling, while Honey jumped up on the porch and sat down by Miss Julie. Willie

Nelson crawled onto my tummy and purred.

"Miss Julie?"

"Yes, dear?"

"You're a really good friend." Even though she was getting old, Miss Julie was a true friend who had never let me down.

"Thank you, dear. I feel the same way about you."

"So tell me this. Am I crazy?"

I expected her to sympathize and tell me I was perfectly normal, just going through some teen-age troubles, but instead she started laughing.

"It's not funny, Miss Julie." I sat up in frustration. "I need to know if I'm nuts or not."

"I'm sorry, sweetie, but it *is* funny!" She hugged her dog.

"Why is it so funny?" I folded my arms and glared at her.

"Because, Piper, we're all crazy."

"What do you mean? Like insane? Needing to be locked up?" I had never, ever heard Miss Julie talk like this, or giggle so much.

"Not mentally unbalanced. Crazy in the goofy sense of the word. Crazy in a fun, nutty way. What I mean is we all have issues, quirks, habits, little oddities that make us seem strange to others. Every one of us. It's what makes people unique to themselves. I began to realize that when I was a teacher, and I've never seen anyone that wasn't nuts in some way." She smiled as she said it.

"You're not crazy. How are *you* crazy?"

"I'm a goofy little old lady who talks to her pets as if they were people, don't I, Honey? And I believe that every problem in the world can be solved by serving cookies with lemonade or iced tea. I'm seventy-three, I've all but adopted a teen-age boy, *and* I'm best friends with a fifteen-year-old girl. Some people would say I should be locked up."

I had to smile at that. She was the least crazy person I could think of.

"But, do you think I'm as wacko as Cassie? She put on a nice face for everyone else and was just horrible to Jeff when no one was around. I don't want to be like that."

"Oh, lord, Piper, you could never be like that. She was badspit freaky insane. You're too honest."

"I just kind of blew up at Jeff, and I've been snotty to Jackie this week, ignoring her and not talking to her."

"I think what you're worried about is the fact that you have a temper and sometimes it goes off suddenly. And you're dealing with feelings that are new to you. But you don't have that meanness in you that Cassie had. Maybe you should think hard about your feelings. Was Jeff only telling you the truth when you asked? Did Jackie really do anything to earn your mistrust? Did you give them both the benefit of the doubt? You have to make up your own mind about people and not take someone else's word for things. But do it fairly, so you can live with your feelings. The fact that you feel guilty about how you've treated Jeff and Jackie proves you're *not* like Cassie. And Piper, my friend, you are a better person than that or we would not even be friends. I may be nice to everyone but I'm picky about who my friends are."

I realized that I had some hard thinking still to do. Since all I had done earlier was brood about how ticked off I was, I figured the best place to think was on the back of a horse.

"Thanks, Miss Julie," I said. "I'll think about all that."

Not wanting to mess with Dotty's little bucking habit, a horse's craziness, I called to Nickel, who came to me right away, and led him into the barn. Of course, he had rolled in the sticky mud after I groomed him before, so I had to brush him all over again before I could saddle him.

It was still early in the day when we left the barnyard and trotted down the lane into the fields. The wonderful smells of green growing things and warm horse rose up to my nostrils. I slowed Nickel to a walk, closed my eyes for a minute and let the sun hit my face. Breathing deeply, I asked myself, what was Jackie really like? We had gotten along well at first. Could we be friends after all? Had I truly been unfair to her and to Jeff? If so, I was a horrible person.

And Jeff...I knew he really did like me and wanted to go out with me. We had been good friends and I never knew a boy before that I could talk to. Why did I let jealousy take over at the movie? I wanted to think honesty was important, but then when Jeff gave me an honest answer, I couldn't deal with it.

Being straight with yourself is hard work. I finally sighed and steered Nickel back toward the barn. My stomach growled, but it didn't feel as bad as when it had the knot in it. I knew I had an apology to make, and it felt good to know what I had to do.

Nickel was very happy to go back to the barn, as horses always are. He picked up his head, turned his good eye homeward and trotted faster. Some horses get "barn sour" where all they want to do is turn around and go back home. This was a good-natured horse, though, who cheerfully went wherever I asked him. I remembered riding through the thunderstorm the night I rescued him. He was steady as a rock. What was his craziness? I hadn't found it yet.

"Nick, old son, you're a good friend," I said, patting him on his grey freckled neck. He snorted in response and let out a high whinny in the direction of the barn. An answering whinny came back to us, probably from Dotty.

"Yeah, they're waiting for you. It's good to have friends."

I was starving by the time I got home for lunch, so I made a peanut butter sandwich, grabbed a glass of milk and crashed in front of the television. I was changing channels, trying to decide between a reality show about buying houses in Mexico and a cooking show featuring spring salads. The doorbell rang and since I hadn't seen Mom around anywhere, I got up to answer it.

Jeff stood on the front porch in a filthy tee shirt and jeans, twitching his hands as if he was trying to dust them off.

"What happened to you?" I said.

"Oh, I've been cleaning out the science lab. Mr. Simpson told me to go get lunch and come back in a few hours."

"On the weekend?"

"Yeah, well, he asked me if I would mind working today, and I said it didn't matter to me." Jeff shrugged.

"Did you eat?"

"No, I came straight here. Piper, I…"

"Just come in," I said, pulling him through the door. "Do you want a PB and J?"

"Well, sure." I had never known Jeff to turn down food. I walked back into the kitchen and began assembling his sandwich. He washed his hands, then sat at the white wooden table and watched me.

"Piper, I need to say something."

"Please let me say this first. I was a terrible person last night. That's not who I want to be. I want us to be honest with each other and then I punished you for saying the truth. I'm sorry, Jeff. I ruined our Friday night and I'm really, really sorry!" I had to brush the water away from my eyes as I put his food in front of him. Turning, I got a cold Coke from the refrigerator and handed it to him. "If I ever act like that again, please remind me that honesty is the important thing." Would he forgive me? Would he even want to go out with me again?

Jeff sighed a huge sigh and sat back in his chair. "Now I don't need to say what I was going to say."

"What were you going to say?"

He shook his head and smiled. "Doesn't matter now."

"But I want to know."

"Uh, uh," he said, shaking his head, but smiling bigger.

"C'mon! Tell me! I can take it." I stood in front of him with my chin out.

Jeff sat forward in his chair. "It was about how you asked me a question and I had to be able to tell you the truth, or this friendship wouldn't work. I can't be your...friend and go out with you if I can't be honest. I was going to say I don't want to live like that. But now I don't have to." He searched my eyes. It dawned on me that I had come close to blowing it completely and my apology was just in time.

"I don't either," I said. "I hate it when people lie about stuff."

"So, just the truth between us? Always?"

"Always," I agreed.

"Then, Piper? I hate peanut butter and jelly."

"Seriously? You're crazy!" Relieved and giggling, I told Jeff about Miss Julie's theory of craziness while I got him a bologna sandwich, which he said he preferred, but no mustard, please. We laughed and talked until he decided he needed to get back to the school and clean the lab some more. He promised to call me later when he was done and maybe we could hang out together.

"Jeff, can I tell you something that's the truth?"

"Of course, what?" He got serious and a wrinkle appeared between his eyes.

"You really smell bad and if you're coming over again, you need to take a shower."

He laughed loudly then. "You know what, Pipe?"

"No, what?"

"I was really bummed when I came over here. I need a new transmission for my truck and can't pay for it, plus I thought I was going to have to break up with you."

Break up? That meant he thought we were going together. We were an item! I stared stupidly.

"But now it's only a new tranny. I've never had any money, so I can deal with that."

Jeff winked and grinned as he left the house. I smiled and closed the door behind him, thinking of all that I had missed out on, back when I hated boys.

Chapter Nine

~ Repairs ~

Later that day, Dad called me and said he wanted to talk to me about the horses. I said I was on my way over anyway. There was something I wanted to talk to him about, too.

When I got to his house, Dad got right to the point.

"Piper, Eric says he called his old clinic and he's treated Daisy before, when he was practicing in Louisville. She was chronic for colic. Do you understand what that means?"

"Well, I know it's not good."

"In this case, it's more than not good. It means you may not be able to sell her. You'll have to tell the people who buy her about her history and not too many people would pay good money for her then."

"Jeez, Dad! Really? I have to tell them?"

"Well, some people wouldn't, but it's not the honest way to do business. Dancer is fine, though. He's a nice-looking colt and probably worth some money."

"So what do I do? All the cards that I put up are gone already. There were seven and people have taken them."

"Have any of them called you?"

"No, and I can't figure out why not."

"I guess you'll just have to wait and see if someone calls, and be honest about it if they do."

"Oh, man!" I slumped in my chair. "This will kill Jeff. He needed the money Daisy would have gotten him, and now he has to get a new transmission for his truck. He was counting on me to sell her."

Dad hugged me. "I know, hon, but you have to tell him. He will need to keep an eagle eye on her. Colic horses have to be watched so they don't get bad."

"Dad? Jeff and I have an agreement that besides me trying to sell Daisy, I will take care of her. He has to concentrate on school so he can get a scholarship."

"Piper, that's a big responsibility."

"You don't think I can do it? Just tell me what to do."

"Of course I think you can do it. And I will tell you everything you need to do. But I also realize that you're fifteen, while Jeff is seventeen. He's just a little older than you are."

"And he doesn't care much about horses, but I do. I'm the one that feeds Daisy and Dancer, brushes them, everything." Did he not remember that I was the caretaker of four horses already?

"Are you ready to go out there every day and limit her feed and walk her around and even put her up in her stall when necessary?"

"Of course! I already go out there every day. You know I'm responsible." Didn't Dad know by now that I took good care of my horses?

"Well, I think I should explain all this to Jeff so he knows what's going on. Eric is having Daisy's records sent from his former practice, so we have them here. I'll let you know when they get here."

"Okay, Dad," I said, still ticked off. Why did he not think I could handle this? If I was responsible about anything, it was horses.

Sunday morning, bright and early, I was at the barn brushing my

66

horses, remembering the night before with Jeff. He had come over with his guitar. He played some blues for me and taught me the words to "Stormy Monday". We watched an old Clint Eastwood movie on TV, made fudge, and it was like nothing had happened, except we understood each other better now.

Addie's mother had taken her to see an old college friend who also had a daughter, so I was by myself that day. I planned to ride Nickel later on—but decided to wait until I had the stalls clean. That's one thing I hadn't realized about horses when I wanted one so badly. They poop in their stalls and then the stalls have to be cleaned. It's not healthy for horses to stand around in mucky pine shavings. I had to prove to my dad that I could take care of horses. So there I was with a wheelbarrow, shoveling out Dotty's stall, when I heard a truck pull in the barnyard. A door slammed and when I looked up, there were Doc Eric and Jackie coming in the barn.

"Hello, Piper," said Dad's new partner.

"Hi," I said, looking from him to his daughter, who looked amazing in jeans and a periwinkle tee shirt.

"Hi, Piper," she said.

"I brought the records from that mare's previous vet in Louisville. We had to contact a former owner to get permission, but they said it was okay. You were right. They lost her to someone in a poker game. Felt real bad about it and they were glad the horse landed in a good place."

"Yeah, except Jeff needs to sell her," I said.

"That may be a problem." Doc Eric scratched his head. "Not many people want to pay good money for a colicky horse. Is Jeff around? Your dad thought I should explain it to him."

"He's in the house studying," I said. Doc Eric turned and left, leaving me and Jackie standing there.

"May I help?" she said.

"Well, sure, I guess," I said. People hardly ever volunteer to help cleaning stalls, so I accepted gladly. I found a manure fork for her and showed her how to fork up the little round balls of manure and put them in the wheelbarrow. When it was full, we would roll the wheelbarrow out and dump it all in a pile by the end of the barn. Miss Julie used it in her garden as the best fertilizer ever. We worked in silence for a few minutes. Then I had to ask.

"So, when the junior boys got in that fight at school, what was that about?"

"I do not know. One boy said something rude to me, I do not remember the phrase, and the other boy hit him for saying it. I was glad the second boy was trying to help me, but the hitting scared me." Jackie hung her head. "Piper, I had to go to the office and talk to Mrs. Harris. I was so embarrassed."

Mrs. Harris was the principal that didn't tolerate bad behavior. Wow.

"So what did Mrs. Harris do?"

"She was actually very nice, once I explained things. She said to try and ignore what I could and be friends with those who were friendly."

"Wow!" This information called for assistance. I knew by now, that I would have to try to be nice and help Jackie out at school. "Would you like to go for a ride with me?"

"Oh! I would love it! I am even wearing my jeans! Let me run up to Mrs. Julie's house and tell Papa!" She sprinted up to the house like a gazelle. That girl could move. Still, I hoped Jeff wasn't watching.

While Jackie told her dad, I went out to catch Nickel and Daisy, figuring if she liked Quarter Horses so much, she should ride one. Daisy kept walking away from me, so I couldn't catch her. I put a halter on Dotty instead, not wanting to waste time chasing an unwilling horse right then. I had the horses all saddled by the time Jackie got back. As she walked back from the house, she stopped a minute to watch Daisy and Dancer in the pasture. We mounted up, me on Dotty and Jackie on Nickel again. Dotty got her craziness out by bucking a little, and we rode into the spring pasture. I clicked at Dotty, making her trot. Nickel and Jackie followed behind us, trotting too. Nickel's legs were longer, so they passed us as we came over the top of a hill. Jackie pulled Nickel back to a walk and turned around to smile at me.

"This is fun, Piper, and I am glad I do not have to ride Dotty. I would be afraid of her bucking."

"Yeah, that's why we got Nickel. Addie was afraid of it, too."

"She seems to be very nice."

"You know, Jackie," I said, "maybe I should go with you next time you shop for sweatshirts or clothes in general."

"That would be nice, Piper. I am stupid about clothes, and the people at school do not like me. I am tall and awkward. I don't fit in here."

"Jackie—you have beautiful clothes. They just aren't what the other kids wear."

"I always wish I had clothes like yours. My mother took me shopping for school in New York City and I had to wear what she bought me. She would not listen to my opinion and wanted me to be stylish. And my papa said I had to wear them. But I bought some blue jeans for riding and a sweatshirt."

"Yeah, you did." I would have to talk to her about that old-lady kitten sweatshirt.

"I love American things. I love the Western look like you wear, and cowboys and Quarter Horses. You are so lucky!"

She wanted to be like me?

"I know Addie would love to go, too. She's a champion shopper." I wasn't sure I wanted to do this, but it seemed like the right thing to do.

Chapter Ten

~ The Snake ~

Sunday night, I texted Addie:

U THERE?
YUP
MADE UP WITH JEFF. ALL MY FAULT. ADMITTED I WAS
NUTS.
U R NUTS. ALL GOOD NOW?
YUP +MAYBE FRIENDS WITH JACKIE.
AWESOME
MAYBE WE TAKE HER SHOPPING?
I'M THERE ALREADY!

A minute later, my phone rang. Addie wanted to find out in detail what happened with both Jeff and Jackie. I explained it all. Addie agreed with me that Jackie deserved a chance. We decided to go shopping with her as soon as possible and get her some new clothes.

When I saw Addie at school on Monday, we found Jackie and all agreed to go shop that afternoon. It was silly for Jackie to waste one more day in those weird, dressy clothes. So that's why Addie, Jackie and I were in the lobby after school was out. As we left the building, Kimmy slunk up to us with her entourage.

"Hey, y'all, where are you going?" she said, looking at the three of us like she knew a secret.

"We're going for a Slurpie Slosh, Kimmy."

"Hmmm, and then what?" Addie and I looked at each other, knowing not to tell Kimmy.

"Don't know yet," said Addie, "We're just going to hang out."

"We're going shopping!" said Jackie with an unsuspecting smile. I knew Kimmy the Snake was up to something, but I didn't know what yet.

"Shopping?" Kimmy smirked. "I hear there's a big sale on office clothes and prom wear at Dillard's. Maybe you can get some school clothes." She looked around at her posse and they all giggled. Jackie stared down at her brown suit with the matching print blouse, a red flush growing on her face.

"Kimmy, that's mean," I said. "She has to wear these things because it was all her mother would buy for her in New York. Her mom is French and doesn't know what kids here wear to school. We're going to go get her some things she'll be more comfortable in."

Kimmy's friends looked at her uncertainly.

"Well," said Kimmy, "I can see she has you two fooled. I guess I don't need to waste my time with you anymore." Kimmy stalked off, her group trailing behind, murmuring to themselves.

"I don't understand. She is against me still, and now she is not your friend anymore?" Jackie's eyes filled with tears. "I am so sorry to cause trouble. Maybe when I have new school clothes she will be nicer."

I put an arm around her as we went down the main steps. "Addie and I have gone to school with Kimmy since we were nine. Kimmy has been mean all her life and always will be," I said. "She's a bully—that's what she is. You just can't let her push you around."

"I was afraid if I was not nice to her everyone would think I was the mean one."

"That won't happen. You should stand up to her. Right, Adds?"

"You bet," said Addie. "Let's go shopping."

The shopping trip was a big success. We went to Moore's, a local clothing store that I like a lot. While Jackie didn't know much about how American kids wear clothes, she had a great eye for color. Her dad had given her a credit card to use, with stern instructions on her limits. Since Addie was the fashionista, I was going to step back and let her pick out clothes for Jackie. But Jackie said, "Piper, I want clothes just like you wear. I love your blue jeans and Western shirts."

I felt easy enough with Jackie by then to tell her not to wear the pink kitten sweatshirt to school. I explained that it would be fine for dirty jobs, but that it really did look like an old lady top. She laughed and said she could turn it inside out, if that would be better, and I thought it would.

In the end, we bought jeans, Western shirts, shorts, t-shirts and a couple of vests that Jackie said "looked just like the cowboys' vests." We went to Taylor's Shoes and found some Western boots for riding and some flip flops for when it got hot. Doc Eric had rented a house not far from Addie's. We walked Jackie home and sat in her pretty yellow bedroom for two hours, laughing and talking about anything and everything. She turned out to be pretty normal, in fact, pretty much like me and Addie. She loved horses and music. Her parents were not together anymore and she lived mostly with her mother. She thought the boys at school were pretty dumb, but unlike me and Addie, there wasn't a mean bone in her body. She didn't even say anything bad about Kimmy.

When I went over to Dad's the next night for Tuesday Tuna Casserole, he gave me a list of what I needed to do for Daisy. I had to make sure she always had plenty of hay and exercise. He wanted me to watch her every day. He said we should worm her regularly, starting that week, and let him know if there was ever anything that seemed odd in her behavior.

"Odd like what?" I asked.

"Like staying off by herself, not eating, no energy—stuff like that," said Dad, putting the casserole in the oven. Had she done any of that? Was not wanting to get caught a symptom? I asked that question and he said no, but she might go off by herself.

"What would it look like if she did get bad?"

"She would look uncomfortable. She might pace around, get up and down, and even hunch her back."

"Jeez, then what should I do?"

"Just call me," he said. "And let's hope that doesn't happen. Honey, I'm counting on you to take care of that mare. She's a special case that really only an experienced horseperson should be dealing with. Although I guess better with you than Jeff."

"Remember, I'm the one that watched her when she was ready to foal," I said.

"I know, and you did a great job there. I'm just saying this could kill her if it's allowed to get bad."

"How would it kill her?"

"Colic makes a horse's gut hurt from manure that can't pass through. They're basically constipated. If it hurts badly enough, they will get down and roll, which can twist their intestines. It's called a torsion. Then nothing can pass through and it takes a long time, but they die painfully."

"Jeez, isn't there anything you can do?"

"You can try and make the manure go through, but if the horse has a torsion, the only way to help it is with surgery."

"Does that work?"

"Sometimes. Surgery on a horse is difficult and expensive. We can't do it at my clinic—we have to send them to a clinic in Lexington where they are set up for horse surgeries."

Scary stuff. I ate the tuna and had some of Dad's brownies for dessert. They were yummy, but I kept worrying about Daisy. What if she got sick again? What if I couldn't keep her healthy? I would be letting Jeff *and* my dad down.

Wednesday morning at school, I bumped into Jeff in the hallway. We rarely see each other at school, since he's two years ahead of me.

"Hey, Piper! How's it going?"

"I'm good, but I'm worried about Daisy. Did Doc Eric tell you about her colic?"

"Yeah, that's a bummer, but I know she's in good hands." He smiled at me with that Jeff grin that made me have butterflies.

"I'll really have to watch her—I'm gonna go out there twice a day."

"How can you do that and get to school on time?" Good point. I shrugged and felt silly.

"At least you have good intentions," he said and laughed. I didn't think he was taking all this seriously enough, and started to say so, when someone bumped into me.

"Oops! Sorry, Piper," said Kimmy Smith as she rubbed my shoulder. "I don't know what I was thinking." She looked at Jeff, smiled with her lips pursed, evidently thinking she looked cute that way. I thought it made her look like a goldfish.

Jeff stared at her with an odd expression on his face. Did he think *she* was cute?

"Well, I need to get to my English class. See you later, Pipe. Bye, um Kimmy, is it?" Jeff turned and started down the hall, away from me.

The Snake giggled, tossing her blond hair, which was curly today, and put a manicured hand on his arm. "You *know* it's Kimmy, silly. But are you going to the North Wing? I'm headed that way, too!

Coincidence? I'm gonna tag along with you to the gym—I have cheerleading practice. 'Bye Piper, Honey!"

Turning her back on me with a little smirk, she tucked her hand into Jeff's arm and strutted off beside him, chattering to him. What was that about? What was Kimmy after, besides Jeff, obviously? Why was she trying to make me jealous? I thought about it the rest of the day.

Since I remembered that Daisy was off by herself a day earlier, I hurried out to the farm after school. Dotty, Nickel and Dancer were grazing under the big oak tree in their pasture, but Daisy wasn't to be seen. Concerned, I hurried into the barn and found her in her large foaling stall that Sam had built last fall.

"Hey, Sis," I said, the way my dad talked to nervous horses to calm them. "What are you doing in here by yourself?"

Daisy's head was down like she was sleeping, but an eye was open as she followed my movements into the stall with her.

"Daisy, Daisy," I sang to her, coming around and patting her shoulder. I offered her a handful of oats that I had scooped up on the way in. She sniffed them and turned her head away. I persisted and she finally stuck her nose into my palm and nibbled. I rubbed her forehead and patted her neck.

She moved away from me and stepped out the door into the pasture. Whew! For a minute, I was scared, but she seemed okay then.

I putzed around the barn, cleaning stalls, brushed Nickel and Dotty and after washing my hands, I walked up to the house. Someone must be home because Jeff's truck and Miss Julie's car were parked outside. I could see through the screen door into the house, so they had not gone away and locked the heavy wooden door.

"Hello?" I called in the screen door, peeking into the kitchen.

"Hey, Pipe, come on in." Jeff was at the kitchen table with a notebook and chemistry text spread out in front of him.

"Is this where you do all your homework?" I asked.

"Yeah, except for reading. I don't have a desk up in my room and don't want to spend money on one right now."

"Chemistry? Is it hard?"

"Yes, it's hard! Hardest class I have." Jeff sighed and slumped in his chair.

"Is Miss Julie home?" I had something to ask him, but I didn't want anyone else around when I did.

"She went with Sam to shop for something. She said she'd be home by 5:30 to cook supper. Did you need to talk to her?"

"No," I said, "I need to talk to you." I sat down and stared across the table at him. Now was my chance to find out how he felt about Kimmy.

"Here I am. Have at it." He smiled at me, with that smile that made my stomach flip over.

"Remember when we said we'd tell the truth to each other?"

"Of course. What?" Jeff leaned forward as his face got serious and his eyes searched mine.

"Well, it's about Kimmy. Do you think she's pretty? Or cute?"

"Who?"

"Kimmy. Kimmy that walked down the hall with you this morning. Kimmy that threw herself all over you!"

"Oh, her." He started laughing. Honest, he doubled over laughing.

"What's so funny, Jeff? I asked you what you thought of her."

Still giggling, Jeff sat up and looked in my eyes. "Kimmy is the last girl in the world I would think was pretty. She's totally fake, from her bleached hair to all her makeup to her painted nails. That wouldn't be so bad, but she's not an attractive person inside either."

Oh, relief! "What do you mean?" I asked, pretending I didn't know.

"She's a backstabber. She pretended to be your friend, but you

76

should have heard the things she said about you and Addie."

"Like what?"

"I won't repeat them. I ducked away this morning as quickly as I could and left her standing in the middle of the hall. Mr. Miller will think I'm nuts crashing into his math class for only two minutes and then ducking out again when the hallway was clear. No, I think it's safe to say that Kimmy is an ugly person. A real turn-off." Jeff was still chuckling. "Not like Jackie."

Jeff poured me some of Miss Julie's famous lemonade then. So Jackie was a turn-on? Hmmm. I didn't know how to deal with that, but I drank the lemonade.

Chapter Eleven

~ Walking ~

Thursday morning went by like any other. I saw Jeff in the hall and waved at him. He smiled back with that killer grin, but then stared at Jackie as she came up to me before English class. He walked away, and I started to call to him but changed my mind, went in and sat down. The old jealousy was flaring up again. She was just too pretty and he couldn't keep from looking at her. I felt like dogmeat next to her. I couldn't bring myself to say anything to her all day.

After school, I went home, got my bike and rode out to the farm to do my daily horse check. I leaned my bike against the barn and walked through the wide door, watching the swallows swoop and dive through the opening. There were nests up in the rafters now. Later in the summer I would be able to see babies peeping out. The stalls were all empty except for Daisy's. She was in it again, very still, with her head down.

"Oh, dear, are you not feeling good? It will be okay, Sis." I crooned to Daisy, keeping her and myself calm. This time I couldn't get her to eat any oats or the minty horse treats they all loved. She stood still, with her head down. No sign of interest in anything. A very bad sign. I needed to call my dad right away.

I picked up my phone and called the clinic, heart racing. No signal. I hated that sometimes I couldn't get a signal at the farm. It was annoying always, but especially bad when you have horses that need prompt medical attention. I stepped outside the barn and tried to call from there.

Sometimes getting away from the building worked. Again, no signal. Leaving Daisy in her stall, I trotted up to the house.

"Hey! Miss Julie! Jeff! Are you home?" No answer. I tried again. The backdoor was closed.

"Anybody home?" I knew they probably weren't because neither the blue Cougar nor Jeff's truck was parked outside. Miss Julie always told me it was okay to go in and use her bathroom, so I knew she wouldn't mind me using her land line phone either. She told me where she left the key so I could let myself in. I found it, opened the door, and entered the big airy kitchen.

Dialing quickly, I called Dad's cell phone, but it went right to voice mail. He was talking on it. I let out a heavy breath of frustration and phoned the clinic.

"Hello? Veterinary Clinic, this is Sue."

"Sue! It's Piper. I need to talk to my dad." I was speaking too quickly, but my mouth was dry and I only had one thought: get help!

"Oh, I'm sorry, honey. He's over in the next county blood testing cattle. He's out of range and won't be back till tonight."

"I think Jeff's horse is colicking. What should I do?" At this point, my mouth was dry and my heart raced.

"Let me go ask Eric. He's in surgery. I'll see if he can stop."

"Sue, he can't leave in the middle of surgery."

"Can I call you back?"

"I don't think my phone will get a signal. But try, okay?"

"Okay, Piper, but it's a pretty long surgery. I don't know how long it will be."

"Just try, okay? Tell him what's going on."

I hung up and ran back to the barn, hoping the signal would go through when Sue or Doc Eric did call me. Maybe he would get done and just drive out to the farm.

Daisy was in her stall, moving restlessly. Her sides and neck were sweating. What was I going to do? I watched and worried, worried and watched. I got a bucket of water and offered some to Daisy, but she turned her head away. I knew from my dad that it's not a good sign when horses just stand still and sweat and that's all she did. Her head hung down, eyes dull, and she sweated.

I kept looking at the big clock on the barn wall. It had been fifteen minutes. Why didn't he call? How long did that surgery have to go anyway? I jumped when I heard a sound at the barn door and Jackie walked in, panting.

"Piper, I was at the clinic when you called. My papa cannot come, but he gave me directions for what to do. I tried to call you, but you did not answer."

"My phone isn't connected. What did he say?" Not great relief, but at least I had some communication from the clinic.

"He said to put a halter on her and walk her. He said to walk, walk, walk and, above all, whatever we do, *not* to let her lie down and roll."

"That's it?"

"He said she is sweating because she is in pain. Poor thing! See how much she sweats." Jackie put a hand on Daisy's flank, but the horse didn't seem to feel it. She turned and looked at her belly for about the tenth time.

"Poor baby," I said. "She must be looking at her belly because it hurts so much. She did that when she was foaling, too." Tears came to my eyes as I thought about the pain she was in.

Walking her didn't sound like much, but grateful for something to do, I grabbed Daisy's halter, slipped it over her head and buckled it. Hooking a lead rope to it, I led her out into the barn aisle and started to walk. She resisted at first, hunching her back a little, but then followed me.

"Did your dad say anything else?"

"He explained to me what happens with colic."

"Yeah, my dad did, too."

"He says to keep walking her and call him again if Daisy poops. That is all he said. But he told me I should hurry when I came to tell you. If she poops, she will be all right." Jackie wrung her hands as she talked.

So I walked that horse up and down the barn aisle, turned around, walked some more. Jackie sat on a hay bale and watched. Once, Daisy pulled back and started to lie down.

"No! Papa said she must *not* lie down!"

"Oh, jeez! There she goes. Help me, Jackie!" Daisy was not a large horse, but she still must have weighed a thousand pounds. Not a light little load. Together we pushed on her back and pulled on her halter until she got up and began walking again. We both petted and praised Daisy, but didn't let her stop to think about lying down again. The day was getting warm and I took off my Fighting Salamanders sweatshirt. I cooled off and felt better with just a tee shirt. Soon I needed a drink of water, so Jackie took over, walking Daisy up and down in the same rhythm.

After a while, she broke the silence. "Piper, may we talk?"

"What about?"

"I know you do not like me."

"Oh, but I…" This was very awkward.

"No, please, let me say this while I have courage. I know you do not like me and it bothers me very much. I do not know what I have done to cause this, but if you will tell me what it is, I will try to fix it."

I stared at her as she walked Daisy, thinking I had never, ever had anyone ask for help with such bravery. Taking a deep breath, I said, "It's my fault. You are…just beautiful and you have a great figure. That's why."

"I do not understand."

"Of course you don't. You haven't done anything wrong."

"Then why are you so mad at me? You do not talk to me, you walk away. I thought we were friends when we went shopping, but then you got mad again and quit talking to me. I do not understand."

"I'm jealous, okay? Like I said, it's all my fault." I felt dumb admitting this, but was really glad to get it off my chest.

"Why are you jealous?"

I walked over and took Daisy's halter to take a turn walking, trying to decide how to answer her.

Jackie sat on a hay bale looking hopeful. "I have a confession, Piper. I am terribly shy. My papa is always pushing me forward and making me do things. I hate it. I cannot just laugh and talk to people, so I keep quiet and hope someone will talk to me."

"Does it work?" I asked.

"No, people think I am a sneerer. Sneerer, is that a word?"

"You mean stuck-up?"

"Yes! People believe I am a stuck-up and not interested, when I am afraid to talk to them."

Now I felt even more terrible because I was one of the ones who had believed that about her.

"Come on, Daisy, walk, walk, walk," I whispered. Jackie heard me and nodded. She joined in chanting, "Walk, walk, walk!" I handed Daisy back to Jackie when I got tired and needed a drink. We offered Daisy a drink of water from a rubber bucket, but she turned her nose away. We walked again, up and down the aisle of the barn.

Time passed. I checked the clock in the barn every so often.

"Please listen, Jackie. I'm really sorry. I've been so jealous of you because Jeff thinks you're so good-looking. I don't want to be like that and I want to be friends."

"Oh, Piper! Of course! I was hoping for that. But, you and Jeff have this...friendship of the heart?"

"I guess so." I still wasn't sure what to call what Jeff and I had.

"I would never, never come between a friend and her boyfriend. Jeff is a nice guy, but he will be like a brother to me. I swear it." Jackie said this so fiercely that I believed her.

"That's good enough for me," I said as I took the lead from her and began walking Daisy again.

We must have talked for another hour. I told Jackie the story again about Addie and me rescuing Dotty from Ugly Jake, then about saving Nickel from the gang that tried to rob Miss Julie. Then I told her how Jeff and I had helped Daisy have her baby last fall. Jackie told me a story about when she was a little girl and her dog got hit by a car. She took it to a vet and it only had a bruised shoulder. We had been walking back and forth for what seemed forever, when Daisy stopped dead still, lifted her tail, and pooped a great big pile of manure onto the barn floor. I had never been so glad to hear that sound and smell that smell in my life.

"Wow!" I cheered. "That must be a good thing!"

"Should I call my papa?"

"I guess so, if he said to. I couldn't get through earlier." I said, giving her my phone, since she didn't have one. She dialed quickly and gave me a thumbs-up when it connected on the other end. *Now* it went through!

"Sue, may I speak to my papa, please? This is Jackie. Thank you." Jackie looked at me with huge eyes. "Papa? I am in the barn with Piper and Daisy, the mare. We have walked her and she has pooped."

She handed it back a minute later.

"He just got out of his surgery. He is leaving now and is on his way out and will be here soon. He said to keep her on her feet, but we can stop walking her."

"Thank goodness."

Keeping her on her feet was no problem, since Daisy now acted like there had never been a problem. Her eyes were bright again and she looked around alertly, sniffing at hay. Jackie hugged the mare's neck and whispered to her. We gave her water in the bucket, which she sipped daintily. After about ten minutes, Doc Eric's truck rolled to a stop by the barn door and his tall self emerged from the cab.

He looked around at the two of us with the bay mare.

"How is she?" he asked.

"I think she's cooler, and she seems calmer," I said. "Actually, she seems like she's back to normal."

"Good. When did she poop?" he asked, eyeing the pile in the barn aisle.

"Just now," I said. "Five minutes ago."

"And how long have you been walking her?"

"Since I got here, Papa. Over an hour."

"Well, you probably saved her life, girls."

"So she's going to be okay?"

"For now. Luckily you were both here to walk her and keep her from getting down and rolling."

He had his stethoscope out and was checking Daisy's stomach sounds as Jeff walked in the barn.

"Hi, people! Did I hear Doc Eric say that you saved my horse again?"

I explained what had happened and ended with, "She brought the directions from her dad when my phone couldn't get a signal. We did it together."

"Jackie and you?" Jeff looked from me to her, confused.

"Yep, the two of us." I grinned at him. "But I didn't know you had a bike," I said, looking at Jackie.

"I do not have a bike."

"How did you get here so fast?"

"Well, I ran."

"Wait," said Jeff. "You ran out here to save my horse?"

"Um…yes," said Jackie, with a smile and a shrug. "I used to run on a track team in France."

"Piper, I think we have another Horse Rescuer here." He looked at me to see if I was okay with that.

"We do!" And I was.

Chapter Twelve

~ Fried Chicken and Pecan Pie ~

My head was down on Friday morning when I walked into the school building. I was glad that we had walked Daisy through her bout of sickness. That felt really good, but how was I ever going to sell her for Jeff? She had a hard case of colic and could get sick again at any time. As I thought about selling her, I realized that no one had ever called about the cards. Was someone taking them from the clinic and not wanting the horse? Someone just being mean?

I was early, so I waited by Addie's locker. She usually hurried in right before the bell and we didn't have much time to talk. She had not answered my texts, so I was afraid she lost her phone again.

"Hi Pipe," she said, throwing her purse into her locker and grabbing several books. She slammed and locked it and was taking off down the hall, when I grabbed her arm.

"Wait! What's up? Did you lose your phone again?"

"Duh, yeah! My mom this time."

"Were you texting Joe again?"

"What do you think? I just don't see why they have to be so nosy! Mom said she'll give it back when I promise to forget about him."

"Will you? You know he's too old."

Addie looked at me with flashing eyes. "I don't know if I can. You don't know how much I care about him. And what about you? Jeff is two years older than you are. See you after school, I guess." She huffed off to class, leaving me staring at her back.

"Two is different than five!" I called. "I'll wait for you. I want to tell you about Daisy. And about Jackie."

When school was out, I waited on the front steps for Addie. I decided to call Sue at the clinic and see what she knew about the index cards.

"I'm sorry, Piper, I don't know a thing," Sue said. "The cards are gone. I don't have much time to watch the bulletin board, but I've never seen anyone taking one."

"Do you think someone could be taking them all and throwing them away?" I just couldn't believe that seven or eight cards had been taken, but no one had called me.

"Piper, honey, why would anyone want to sabotage your chances of selling those horses? It doesn't make sense." Sue was always very practical.

"I don't know, but keep your ears open, will you? I *have* to get them sold!"

"Sure will, hon. I didn't know you were so desperate. And I'll tell all my friends. I have a meeting tonight and a couple of them are horse people."

"Great! Just have them call me. Thanks, Sue." I hung up feeling confused, but hopeful.

Jeff walked out, sat down beside me with a pile of textbooks that he said were his weekend plans. Pretty soon, Addie came along and draped herself across a step above me.

"Hey, Pipe. Hey, Jeff. So tell me about Daisy."

It took about five minutes for me to tell Addie all about our walking session in the barn, about Jackie running out from town with the information that saved Daisy's life. Jeff chimed in about how great we both had been to take care of his horse. He was very grateful to us both.

We had just finished telling the story, when Kimmy came out of the building with her gang of six Kimmy wanna-bes behind her. We waited to see what she was going to do. It didn't take long.

"So Piper, where's your French Dip friend?"

"She'll be here in a minute," I said. "We're waiting for her."

"I'm glad you took her shopping. She looks much more human today!" Kimmy snickered and all her buddies snickered with her. Then she saw Jeff, who sat there taking it all in.

"Well hi, Jeff." She batted big blue eyes at him and smiled a fake model's smile. I didn't worry about her flirting since Jeff had told me what he thought of her. Jeff watched her as if she was an interesting insect.

"Are you hoping to see what the French Dip is like for yourself? I guess some of the Junior boys could tell you a lot about her. But if you want someone that knows her way around, I can give you my phone number." She moved close to him and touched his knee. So Kimmy was getting more aggressive? Jeff looked at me and winked. I smiled.

"Why do you pick on Jackie?" he asked. "She doesn't go out with anyone. She doesn't even flirt, even though most of the guys wish she would." Kimmy stood up straighter. I could almost see her mind working. Here was a boy, a Senior boy and a cute one, one of the most desirable guys in school, challenging her. They usually fell all over themselves trying to please her. Her chin went up.

"I don't pick on her, she does stuff to herself," Kimmy sputtered. "She, she acts weird and everything, doesn't she guys? Guys?" Kimmy looked around at her friends, who were staring at their feet.

Addie spoke up. "You should be nicer to Jackie. She's trying hard and it's not her fault she's been sort of different."

"Oh, she's different, all right. Am I right, y'all?" Again, Kimmy looked around her, but her posse was trying to fade back into the school building. Evidently Kimmy was sometimes wrong.

She stamped her foot. "Come back here!" But the other girls in her crowd had vanished.

"If you can't be nice, you should leave her alone," I said, looking Kimmy straight in the eyes.

Kimmy the Snake looked from me to Jeff to Addie. At that moment, Jackie came out of the big double doors and smiled at all of us.

Kimmy turned without speaking and went inside by herself, leaving the four of us on the steps.

"What has happened?" asked Jackie.

"Oh, a snake realized that it's not as powerful as it thought it was," I said. "Anybody want a Slushy Slosh?" But somehow I didn't think Kimmy would leave it at that. There would be more trouble ahead, and we would have to protect Jackie.

It was windy on Friday night as Dad and I went out to Miss Julie's for dinner. She had called and invited us, along with Doc Eric and Jackie. I knew that Sam and Mom would be there, too and was grateful for the fact that Mom and Dad got along most of the time. And I hoped that Jeff would take his head out of his books and show up. I braided my hair and wore a soft pink cotton plaid shirt. Mom went for neutrals, but I was finding out I liked color.

"Dad," I said in the truck on the way over. "Do you know why Miss Julie is having a special dinner?"

"No, honey," he said. "You know as much as I do."

"Do you think…oh, never mind."

"What? Do I think what?"

"Do you think Mom and Sam will get married? It's not about that, is it?"

Dad was silent for a few minutes. His forehead wrinkled like it does when he's thinking hard.

"I don't think so. I think Jean would tell me before they announced it to the world. But would you be all right with it if they did get married?"

I had been thinking about it for a while and had decided I would be cool with it.

"Oh, sure, but would you?"

Dad laughed. "Honey, I was not able to make your mother happy, so I wish Sam all the best if he can."

"Dad, do you ever think you'll want to date again?" I loved being able to talk with him about important things.

Dad looked at my face as we pulled into Miss Julie's long, gravel driveway.

"Sometimes I want to, but then it just seems like I don't have any time for personal relationships. That was one of the problems when Jean and I were married. Maybe with Eric here, I can have a more balanced life. And now let's go have dinner and see what all the hoopla is about."

When we walked in the kitchen door, closing it against the wind, Jeff was sitting at the kitchen table. He pushed a chair out for me, so I sat down.

"What's up?" I asked.

"Hey, Piper. Hey, Doc," he said. My father sat down beside him on the bench.

Jackie and Doc Eric knocked on the door then, so Jeff got up to let them in. Jackie was a knockout in a red dress with black vines all over it. I discovered I wasn't jealous any more. Jeff might stare at Jackie, but it was me he liked.

"Hello," said Jackie, smiling at me and Jeff. We were pals now. Doc Eric shook hands with the guys and said hi to me.

We all trooped into Miss Julie's living room, where there was more seating. Dad and I sat on the flowered couch. Jeff perched very carefully on the velvet antique chair. Doc Eric found an overstuffed armchair and Jackie balanced on the arm of that.

"Where are Sam and Jean?" Miss Julie came bustling into the room with her dog and cat trailing behind her. "Everyone is hungry but we can't start without them. Yes, I know, Honey! I can feed you anyway. Be right back." She hurried out into the kitchen and we heard her rattling dog and cat food into their dishes.

We all just kind of stared at each other, wondering what was happening. Dad glanced at his watch. "Jean never was too punctual..." he began, as the front door opened and Sam and my mom blew into the room. They stood in front of the fireplace, grinning.

Miss Julie hurried in again.

"Oh good, you're here!" she said with a smile. "I believe we are all ready."

Jeff cleared his throat as he stood up. "I've been accepted at Western Kentucky State, full scholarship." Everyone in the room cheered. He took a deep, shaky breath and smiled at Miss Julie. "It's all because of you, Miss J. Thank you!" Miss Julie took his head in her hands, kissed his cheek and hugged him tight.

"And thank you, Doc and Sam, for the recommendations. I know they helped me get in." Then they all had to shake hands with Jeff and congratulate him. A bubble of happiness grew in my stomach. All the adults took turns hugging him, but I felt suddenly shy and hung back. Everyone went into the dining room for dinner, so I followed. I wanted to say something to him with no one else around.

Miss Julie's dinner was a celebration of comfort food that wasn't good for you, but seemed right for a happy night. She made fried chicken, mashed potatoes, rolls, southern green beans with bacon in them and a pecan pie for dessert. I don't usually eat much but I gorged as much as anyone else. Even Jackie dug in like she didn't care about her figure. Not many people knew that she ate like a horse most of the time.

We had all finished eating and I was clearing the table, when Doc Eric came back into the dining room to look for his phone. He found it by his place and was leaving when I said, "Um, Doc Eric? Could I talk to you for a minute?"

"Sure, Piper, what is it?"

I explained what was in my mind. With a grin, he left to find Jackie and go home.

When everyone else had said goodnight, I stepped out onto the back porch. The wind blew the flower baskets so they looked like they might blow off their hooks.

Jeff came out soon after and sat on the old porch swing beside me, smiling.

"You know," he said. "Sometimes you just have to trust that things will turn out. I can't believe the way this all happened. I meant to thank you in there, too. If you hadn't taken care of the horses, I couldn't have studied so hard. Thank you, Piper. And why do you look like you know a secret?"

"I can't tell you yet, but I believe you have to trust that things will turn out, but you also have to do whatever you can to make them turn out." I turned and looked in his eyes. "Jeff, I'm really glad for you. You deserve that scholarship."

"So, do I get a hug?" he was back to his normal, shy self. I gave him a strong, fierce hug, and at the same time wondered again, would he miss me when he was away at school?

Chapter Thirteen

~ Dancer ~

Saturday morning, I grabbed a banana on my way out to the farm, and rode my bike to make better time. I had stayed at my dad's house last night, since we went to Miss Julie's dinner together. I was in a hurry to see Jeff and tell him again how happy I was that he got his scholarship. I wanted to talk a little about college and how he felt about it. Mostly I wanted to find out if he would miss me.

No one was home at the house, so I went out to visit my little herd. The sun warmed my back as I sat in the grass watching the horses nibbling new spring clover. Red clover flowers are so sweet that I liked to chew them sometimes. They tasted a little like honeysuckle.

The horses heard the truck first, lifting heads and pricking up their ears toward the driveway. Doc Eric's dusty white truck came barreling down toward the barnyard and stopped with a jerk. Jackie jumped out and ran to the gate when she saw me. Climbing over easily and swiftly, she hurried over to me and threw herself on the grass. Her dad followed more slowly.

"Wow, Jackie! You said you were a runner, but I didn't know you were that athletic." She did much better with tennies on than when she wore heels.

"Piper, the most wonderful thing!"

"Well, what?"

"My papa is going to buy Daisy for me!"

I sat up and looked at Doc Eric, who was just arriving in the paddock.

"You did it?" I said, grinning.

"Yes, really! Tell her, Papa!"

"It's true, Piper. I called Jeff and had a long talk last night on the phone. It was actually a no-brainer, just as you said. Jacqueline wants a Quarter Horse, Jeff has one to sell, but it has medical issues. But I'm a veterinarian and Jacqueline loves that mare enough to run to rescue her. We settled on a reasonable price. It's not what he could have gotten if Daisy was healthy, but it's something. Thank you for the idea. You're a good friend to my daughter." We watched Jackie, who had gotten up and walked over to Daisy. The girl and horse were in a world of their own. Jackie was rubbing, scratching, and hugging the mare; Daisy nodding her head in pleasure and chewing the treats Jackie gave her. I didn't need to worry any more about Daisy getting attention.

"That's awesome, Doc. I'm really glad for Jackie." I smiled up at Doc Eric.

"And I want to tell you thank you again, Piper, for being Jacqueline's friend. She is very shy and I'm afraid I got pushy about finding friends for her, making sure they are good students and good people. That's what you are. I think I'm a pretty strict father, since I'm not used to it. I'll have to learn from Dan, since he obviously has done a great job of parenting."

"Thanks. But what will happen when Jackie goes back to live with her mom in France?"

"I will want to see Jacqueline as much as possible, and she will have a horse here for when she comes to visit, so I'm hoping she will come back often. I'll keep Daisy and maybe ride her myself. I'm thinking maybe I could pay you to take care of Daisy when Jackie's gone. You're obviously good with colic horses."

"Sounds good to me," I said. A source of income. Better and better.

I waited around most of the morning, but Jeff was nowhere to be seen. When I called his phone, it went to voice mail. He was either talking a lot or he'd turned it off. Disappointed, I went home and made a sandwich. I was halfway done with it when Mom walked in the front door.

"Piper, when did you get home?"

"About twenty minutes ago. What's up?"

"Well, Sue at the clinic was trying to get hold of you. You must have been out by the barn for your phone not to work."

"Stupid phone signals! What did Sue want?"

"Oh, I'm not sure. Something about a horse." While Mom is very efficient at the law office, she can be vague when it comes to messages for me. I called Sue immediately.

"Piper! I've been calling and calling."

"I know. I'm sorry—not good service out at Miss Julie's. So what's up?"

"I have a friend that is interested in buying that colt of Jeff's. Not the mare though, is that a problem?"

"Oh, my gosh, no!" I said. "Who is it?"

"A friend of mine named Annie. I'll have her call you, okay? I just didn't want to give them your number unless I knew you'd sell the colt by himself."

"Great! Hey, Sue? Did she take one of my index cards?"

"No, I was telling Annie about him when I was at her house last night. Anyway, hang up and I'll have her call you."

So I hung up and finished my sandwich waiting for the phone to ring. It took about twenty minutes but then it dinged.

"Hello?"

"Is this Piper?"

"Yes."

"My name is Annie and I'm a friend of Sue's. She said you had a Quarter Horse colt that was about six months old and for sale."

"That's right," I said, pumping my fist with a grin. "He's not actually mine. I'm helping a friend find a buyer for him."

"What color is he?"

"Um, he's red bay with a star and two white socks. He's really pretty and he moves nicely. His mother is absolutely gorgeous and he'll look a lot like her. She's not for sale, though." I smiled, thinking of Jackie's excitement earlier.

"No, I don't want the mother. I'm looking for a project. I just sold a horse and there's an empty stall in my barn that needs a tenant. I like to train the young ones." Annie laughed. She sounded easy-going and fun. "I need to know two things: who is the sire and when could I come see the colt?"

"The sire is Golden Jet and you can come this afternoon or any time tomorrow."

We arranged that she would come out the next day around 1:00 pm, since she still had riding lessons to give that afternoon. I figured that would give me plenty of time to get hold of Jeff and have him there. I gave Annie directions to Miss Julie's and said goodbye.

I finally got Jeff on his phone Saturday night, late. We talked about Doc Eric buying Daisy for Jackie, and then Jeff got really excited when I told him about Annie coming to look at Dancer.

"Piper, that's great! You're coming out then, too aren't you?"

"You kidding? I wouldn't miss it! And Jeff...I just wanted to tell you again how glad I am about your scholarship. You deserve it."

"Thanks, Piper. But you know what…"

"No, what?" I bit my lip. Could I ask him about college now?

"Never mind, Pipe. I'll see you tomorrow."

"Okay, 'bye!"

Early on Sunday, I got another call.

"Hello?"

"Yeah, is this the gal with the colt to sell?"

"Yes, this is Piper." I put my phone against my chest and whispered to my dad, who was eating fried eggs. "Dad! Someone else wants to look at Dancer. What should I do?"

"Give him a time to come look. Just because Sue's friend wants to look, doesn't mean she'll buy him. He's not sold until you have the check."

"Can you come out today? At 11:00?" I figured that would give the guy time to look at Dancer before the woman got there.

"Yeah, sure, I'll be there." I gave him directions to the farm. He said his name was Mike and he'd be there.

I lay in bed for a long time that night, hoping and hoping that the lady would buy Dancer. She seemed nicer than the man, who sounded rough and rude. But either way, if one of them would buy him, it would help Jeff pay for school and his truck, and it would make Jeff like me better, it would give Dancer a home. What if they both didn't want him? I finally fell asleep, thinking that I was worrying my hair off.

I got there at 10:30 the next morning, let Dancer in a stall and groomed him till he shone. Jeff strolled out and sat around, waiting with me. At 11:00 there was no sign of the man, rough voice or not. By noon, we had decided he probably wasn't going to show.

I went into the house to use the bathroom and when I came out, I saw a brand new, dark red pickup parked near the barn. "Hey, Piper," said Jeff. "This is Annie. I told her that you were the one who always took care of Dancer. You're the one that can answer most of her questions."

"Hi," I said, shaking hands with the short, plump woman. She had a friendly, freckled face and eyes that laughed. She asked a number of questions and I answered them the best I could.

"Do you want to see him move?" I asked, after a while.

"Sure," said Annie, so I put a halter on him and walked him up and down the barn aisle.

Annie ran her hands over his legs, looked in his mouth and patted his nose.

"I think I know everything I need to know," she said. "I've seen him move, I've checked him over and he's healthy. You were right, his mother is a beautiful mare and the sire is a crazy good stallion. Those are wonderful bloodlines. I think if we can agree on a price, we have a deal."

As my heart began to jump with joy, a dirty brown truck barreled into the barnyard. It stopped in front of us and a short, grubby man climbed out of the cab.

"You Piper?"

"Yes," I said, not sure about what to do. "Are you the guy that called this morning? Mike?"

"Yep," he said. "Hey, Annie," he said, looking at her with a squint.

"Mike," she said with her lips pressed tight and her arms folded. So she knew him, but they didn't like each other. Interesting.

"That the colt?" He walked over by Dancer and put his hands on the shiny flank. "Looks good, but I need to see him move. I'm lookin' for a performance horse."

Jeff and I looked at each other and at Annie. I wished my dad was here. I just didn't know the etiquette of this situation and I was pretty sure Jeff didn't either.

The Quarter Horse

"Well, can I see him or not?" Mike was getting impatient.

Annie, seeing our dilemma, stepped in and said, "Sure, go ahead and lead him around. I'll wait."

"You want this horse, too, Annie? You got a claim on him?" Mike spoke softly.

"Not yet," she said.

"Maybe not ever," he said, spitting out the side of his mouth.

To smooth things over, I took Dancer's lead and began to walk him around the barnyard.

"What do you want for him?" asked Mike.

Jeff looked at me and shrugged. I wasn't sure what to ask for either, but my dad told me he was valuable and some words to say.

"He's a valuable colt," I said. "And he hasn't been gelded yet. If you get him to be a great performance horse, he'll be worth a ton—$10,000."

Mike snorted. "I don't think he's worth that, but let me call my brother and see if he wants to chip in some funds. I'll get back to you."

"Then let me make an offer," said Annie. "$15,000. Today." That number was beyond my wildest dreams. I looked at Jeff and nodded furiously.

"Deal," he said, and they shook hands. Mike muttered some cuss words and looked at Annie. "That's twice. One day you'll get what's coming to you, lady." He spat again, climbed into his pickup and threw gravel as he sped down the driveway.

"Is he going to be a problem?" I asked.

"I don't think so, but he is not a nice man," Annie said. "Be glad he didn't get your colt. That's too good a horse for him." She went to her truck, got a checkbook and wrote a check right then and there for the whole amount.

"I live close—only ten miles away. I'll be back with my horse trailer to get him later this afternoon," she said, and drove off in a cloud of dust.

Jeff and I stared at the check, smiling at it, then at each other.

"Put it in the bank," I said. "That's what my dad does when he gets a big check. He deposits it before the people can change their minds."

The drive-up part of the bank was open on Sunday, so Jeff drove the check to town. I got on my phone and called Dad—the call went through this time—and told him about the deal. He was impressed with my horse-dealing, he said, and promised to come out in an hour with some oats he'd bought on Saturday.

Jeff was still gone and Dad and I were unloading some oats for the other horses when Annie came back to get Dancer. She had a beautiful new dark red horse trailer that matched her pickup. My dad raised his eyebrows when he saw the expensive rig pull into the barnyard. Then he raised them higher and smiled when Annie got out of the truck.

"Hi Annie, this is my dad."

"Hi again, Piper. Hello, Dr. Jones. Annie McCabe."

"Are you a McCabe from McCabe Riding Stables?"

"That's me."

"So is it just you, or is it a family business?" Why did my dad want to know that?

"My husband and I started the business. When he died four years ago, I just kept running it myself. I've heard a lot about you from Sue— we're old high school buddies. Nice to meet you, Dr. Jones." Annie shook Dad's hand.

"Call me Dan. Nice to meet you. But only believe part of what Sue tells you. The good part. I'm afraid she's seen me at my worst."

"Trust me, it's all been good. Sue thinks very highly of you, and I was looking for a new vet anyway." Annie smiled at us. "Now how about my new project? I'm itching to get him home."

The Quarter Horse

I had put Dancer in a stall earlier and brushed him head to toe. His red coat shone in the sunshine as I led him out of the barn. Annie took the lead from me and walked him right up to the trailer. He put his nose in the air and whinnied high and long. In a minute, his mother answered his call with her own. Then with a little urging from Annie, he followed her up the ramp and into the trailer calmly and quietly.

"Wow!" Dad said. "Nicely done! He's never been trailered before that I know of. Has he, Piper?"

"Nope," I said proudly, just as if he were my child. Well, in a way, he was. I helped him get born.

"That's a good sign," said Annie, "if he's that easy-going about new things. I train horses and as you know, Dan, they aren't all this easy to load."

"Yeah, really," said Dad, watching Annie climb out of the trailer and close the gate behind Dancer. Watching her very closely.

"So, is Jeff around? I'd like to thank him again."

"He went on an errand into town," I said. "He'll be gone for a while. Can I give him a message or anything?"

"He took the check to the bank, didn't he?" Annie laughed. "I would, too. Just tell him Dancer will have a good home and he can come visit whenever he wants. You can too, if you like. However, Dan, I really hope I *don't* need you to visit!"

Dad laughed. "I hope you don't need me to either, but just call if you want me to." He handed her his business card.

Annie got in her truck then, waved, and drove away. Then it hit me. Oh, my gosh! My father had just been *flirting* with the woman! I stared at him for a minute, trying to understand what I had just heard.

"What are you looking at?" said Dad. "Get those oats out of my truck!"

Chapter Fourteen

~ The Great Splash ~

Monday started out feeling like a let-down after all the exciting things that happened on the weekend. However, it sure didn't end up that way. This is what happened: Addie and I didn't see Jackie before class and I wondered if she was skipping in order to play with her new horse. I didn't suspect anything until I saw one of the Kimmy wanna-bes. We were now calling them *Kimsters* in my English class. She was dressed up in a business suit, with high heels and a purse. Mr. Weiland looked at her like she was nuts, but didn't say anything. Not figuring it out yet, I wondered why she had on that get-up. Then I saw her in the hallway with another Kimster, dressed just as fancily.

At lunchtime, the Kimsters always sat at their own table by the biggest window and yep, there they were. Every one of them was dressed to the nines, like a bunch of church ladies going to a tea, making fun of Jackie's former clothes. They snickered and hooted at every boy that walked past them, using fake French accents. What idiots!

I sat at the other side of the room at a table by myself. I was just thinking I was so glad Jackie wasn't in school that day, when she walked into the lunchroom. I tried to wave and catch her attention. She smiled and came to sit by me, setting her tray on the table.

"Where were you this morning?" I asked.

"I had a dental appointment. I hate missing school," she said. I tried to move on the side of her between her and the window so she didn't see the Kimsters, but then she did. Jackie sat perfectly still with her lunch tray in her hands, face growing pale, then it got red. I felt terrible for her. How could I help her through this?

"It's okay, Jackie. Just ignore them."

"How can I ignore people who are making fun of me? You taught me to stand up for myself. It was you that told me not to let Kimmy push me around. Yes?"

"I did say that. So what do you want to do?" I wasn't going to let Jackie deal with those idiots all alone.

The noise from Kimmy's table got louder and louder. Jackie looked at me, her face still bright pink. She got a twinkle in her eye, smiled and said, "Come on!" She stood, and began walking toward Kimmy. This was not shy, fearful Jackie. This was a new, fierce, bold Jackie. She didn't need me, but I was glad to walk by her side. We neared their table and the Kimsters grew quiet, with only the occasional snort being heard. Jackie held her lunch tray in her right hand, calmly turned and took my tray in her left and stepped close to Kimmy.

"You're mean," she said to the entire table, "Stop being mean!" Then she dumped the contents of the trays on the heads of Kimmy and the girls sitting nearest her. Beef stew, applesauce, cooked carrots and milk cartons spilled all over those girls who looked very surprised.

Jackie took my arm with a grin, spun around and walked us both out the door into the hall before Kimmy and her friends could even start shrieking. Which they did. Loudly. It was great!

Later that day, in the principal's office, I explained to Mrs. Harris why it happened. I told her the whole story of Kimmy's meanness. I told her how Jackie had had enough and I was behind her the whole way. Mrs. Harris said she had heard everyone's side of it and she knew Kimmy well enough to know that she deserved milk on her hair.

Mrs. Harris put her arm around Jackie.

"I'm sorry this had to happen to you. It's not a very pleasant introduction to the U.S. and most of all, Kentucky. I hope you know most of us are better than that."

"Piper and Addie and Jeff have been very good friends," said Jackie. "I will always think of my time here with happiness."

"That's good, because I have to give you both a detention for dumping your lunches on Kimmy. I can't help it—I have rules that I must follow."

"Madam, Mrs. Harris, it was I who threw both lunches on the girls. Piper did not throw anything."

"Mrs. Harris, that's just not fair!" I protested. "Jackie was just standing up to a bully! You know the school district has gotten strict about stopping bullies!"

"I admire your loyalty, both of you, but Piper was an accessory to the action, so she will have to serve detention, too."

Mrs. Harris straightened up and looked at us. "You will report to the after-school detention room today at 3:00."

"For how long?" I asked with my best surly look. I was ready for a full-sized pout, attitude and all. Another example of unreasonable adults.

"You can leave at 3:05," she said with a twinkle in her eyes. "I had to laugh.

"Mrs. Harris, what about the Kimsters?" I asked, smiling that Mrs. Harris had such a good sense of humor.

"Who? Oh, them!" Mrs. Harris grinned. "They will get a week's worth of 2-hour after-school detentions for, let's see…for taunting!"

We sat on the steps after school that day, telling Addie all about the Great Splash, as it was being called all over school. Jackie and I had served our five minutes' detention then ran giggling out of the school.

"I wish I had been there," said Addie. "I would have added my tray to it. Except I only had salad today."

"It is the thought that counts," said Jackie. "I would have welcomed your salad. I could not have done it except I knew that my Horse Rescuer friends would stand behind me. Especially Piper, who told me not to let people push me around." She gave me a big hug, but then looked very serious.

"Piper, I have something to tell you that you will not like."

"What?"

"I am afraid you will not want to be my friend when I tell you."

"Well, what?"

"Please do not hate me. I had a reason for doing it."

"What? For Pete's sake, tell me!"

Jackie took a deep breath. "Piper, it was I who removed the advertising cards from the clinic."

"Huh?"

"What advertising cards?" asked Addie.

"The index cards?" I said. "*You* took them?"

Jackie hung her head. "It was I. I am sorry. I took them all."

"Why, Jackie?" I was mystified.

"I did not want you to sell the horses. I thought if the cards were gone, no one would know about the horses and I would have time to talk my Papa into buying me the Quarter Horse."

Mystery solved. "I wondered why all the cards disappeared, but no one called about the horses. It drove me crazy!"

"Can you ever forgive me?" I stared at my new friend.

"Jackie, there is nothing to forgive. When we need a horse, we do whatever we have to do to get it!" I hugged Jackie, Addie hugged Jackie, and Jackie hugged us back.

"*Now* can we go get a Slushy Slosh?" said Addie. "I'm thirsty."

I told the two of them to go ahead and I would catch up. I wanted to wait for Jeff. Addie looked at me knowingly as the two walked off toward the Dairy Dog. My two good friends. My Horse Rescuer friends.

Jeff walked out the doors and plopped his backpack down beside me, following it with himself.

"Hey, kid, I hear you and Jackie made Kimmy and company run for the hills today." He grinned his Jeff grin and I had to catch my breath.

"Yeah, well, she thought it up. I was just her wing man."

"Good for her, and good for you, too." Jeff stood up and motioned with his head. "Want to start home?"

"Can we go past the Dairy Dog first? Addie and Jackie are there celebrating."

"Sure, I need to give Jackie a pat on the back for what she did."

As we walked, I told him about our five-minute detention. Then I racked my brains, trying to figure out how to get Jeff to talk about college. Western Kentucky State was a two-hour drive from Serendipity Springs and he wouldn't be able to come home very often. Even though he had sold his horses, had a truck and a scholarship, I knew Jeff had to count every penny and gas was expensive. Next fall was a long way away, but it seemed like time was going too fast. Did he even think about it? And were the girls on that campus very cute?

"Piper?"

"Mmm-hmm?"

"I'm really lucky."

"You are, I know."

"When Cassie left me with only the horse and the truck, I couldn't see any future ahead for me. But everyone has helped me so much… I have to believe that if I study hard at school, I can have a great life after all."

"Right. But about when you go to school…"

"See, I'm thinking about what I want to do *after* college, which is huge. Before, I couldn't even think about after high school."

"Yeah, well…"

"I have to decide what I want to do with my life, so I know what to study in school."

"Have you thought much about it?"

"Not really, because I can't get past the one thing that's bad."

"What could be bad? It's a full scholarship—they pay for everything. You have a truck to come and go, you have some money for things you might need. It's all good!"

"Not all good, Piper. You won't be there."

I stopped and stared at him, tears filling my eyes.

"But Jeff, you aren't leaving till next fall."

Right there in the middle of the street, he put his arms around me, so gently.

"You won't be there," he said. "And I don't know what I'm going to do about that."

"So you will miss me?" A huge bubble of happiness rose in my stomach.

"Oh, my God, I'm going to miss you. I don't think I *could* go except it's something that I know I have to do."

Jeff held me by my shoulders at arm's length and stared in my eyes.

"Look, Piper, we have the rest of this semester and the whole summer. I'm not going anywhere until next fall. And even then, I'll be able to come home every few weeks. It's not like I'm going to Asia! Since I have a little cash now, I bought you something for helping me out."

"You bought…? You didn't need to…"

Jeff had pulled a little box out of his pocket. He handed it to me. I opened it and saw a little silver horse on a fine chain.

"Oh! It's beautiful!" More tears filled my eyes as I put it around my neck and fastened the clasp.

"The horse reminded me of Daisy—if it weren't for her, we probably wouldn't be friends. I hope you'll wear it and think about me while I'm gone next year. It was the only thing I could think of that would help."

"I won't ever take it off," I said, smiling up at him.

He put his arm around me as we started walking toward the Dairy Dog. I had never had a boyfriend before, but I discovered I liked it as we walked down the street to join my other friends. We were the Horse Rescuers and the future looked bright.

About the Author

Patricia Gilkerson spent a horse-loving childhood growing up in Kentucky, and finally got her first horse as an adult. She began writing books for children at night after teaching all day. Today Patricia lives on a hobby farm in Minnesota with her husband Jim, and the current count of three horses. Her two children are grown with children and pets of their own, so there are frequently grandchildren and granddogs running around her house. Her hobbies include travel, Irish/Celtic music, scuba diving and reading. Her favorite thing to do is to hang out with family and friends.

Like her on Facebook at Patricia Gilkerson
Check her website at patriciagilkerson.com

Other works by the author at Fire and Ice

The Penny Pony
Nickel-Bred
Turn on a Dime
The Great Forest of Shee
The Horse Rescuers Collection